W9-BAY-112

PIGS MIGHT FLY

NICK ABADZIS
JEREL DYE

Color by Laurel Lynn Leake
and Alex Campbell

New York

A Basic Map of the Pigdom Plains
UPPER WARTHOG MOUNTAINS
WILDBOAR WILDERNESS
HOGSBACK
Groatshog
Dungleith
Lake Tuskforth
Citadel of the Celestial Blue
Great Curly Forest
The Scratchings
Hogsfield
Chompston View Peaks
Snagjaw Pass
Snuffledon
Lake Hogwash
Munchton Blissford
Allfather's Pass
SWINEDON
LOWER WARTHOG MOUNTAINS
PIGD
Shanksbridge
Gorgewood
Grotsbury
Messingsford
PLAI
Sowby
SWILLINGTON
Lake Crawloft
Old Hamton Palace
Muckington Barrows
Swineville
Squiffledo
Piggleswick
The Rind
OINKSBURY
Pigsby Hill
HAMSTEAD
Rind Hall
Feastwich Chompston
Hamstead Heath
Gruntsleigh
GREAT HOGSPORT
Stenchford Meadows
PORT PORKINS
BOARHAMWOOD
Piggadilly Circus
Tusksby
Bumton Castle
HOGSMANE HILLS
Dumplington
Pigwash Sands
Wufford Pinkings
TROTTSVILLE
Snuzzledon-by-Sea
Bingeville
Wigglesworth

Mount Halftusk
Uncharted Territories
MOUNT GREATHOG
PURPLE WARTHOG MOUNTAINS
HOGWEED HILLS
HILLS
Hogsback Moors
Lardswick
Scoffsworth Observatory
Mount Shankthorn
MUTTONBACK MOUNTAINS
Mogforth
Loinsmore
Scoffsworth
Mogloch Dripping
Gluttonford
Higher Buttsworth
Gruntwich Splintings
SLOPCHESTER
Little Nibbledon
Buttsworth
Dungbridge
OM
NS
Snoutbridge
Greater Nibbledon
Mintford Scrumpton
Grottswood Forest
RUMPSTON
Huffton Manor
Stenchby
NOSHFORD
Hogton-on-the-Weir
OINKSHAMPTON
Hockton
Guzzledon
Mudbank Festooneries
Glottsley
Squealstone
Swillburgh
Bonebridge
BAY OF PIGS
Stinksford Bottom
Hogsbreath Island
Wurstbrücken
SCHWEINLAN
Stuffington
SCHWEINDORF
Fryford
Rashby Cracklings
Scrutton Buntford
Stoutbach
New Baconburg
STYBRIDGE
Little Hogsport
Plumpton Dock
Archipelago of Pigkind
N
The Glaze
PEARLY SEA
GOURMANDIE
W
E
Montange de Gloutons
Isle d'Or
Las Bacon
S
Cochonilly
Puerco Enfangado
PORCOS

"Dogs look up to man. Cats look down to man.
But a pig will look us in the eye and see an equal."

—Winston Churchill

COME ON... LIFT...

...LIFT, YOU STUPID THING!
BRMMMMMM RRMMMMM,

C'MON, I KNOW YOU CAN DO IT...LIFT!
BRRRRRRRRMMMMM
YES, YES, YOU'RE NEARLY IN THE AIR...
BRRRMMM

AWW, NOOO...
WHAT D'YOU NEED? A LITTLE ENCOURAGEMENT? A LITTLE MAGIC?
SOMETIMES WE ALL NEED A LITTLE ENCOURAGEMENT...

O ALLFATHER SKYPIG, THE SKY, HIS STY, GIVE US WINGS SO THERE WE MIGHT FLY...

WH--

AAAA--

You're flying!

YES!
THE MARK II PROTOTYPE IS AIRBORNE!

Uh-oh.

OH, BUNNIES!
WHERE'S THE TRICKBOX?

AHA!

GOTCHA...

C'MON
C'MON

NOT TOO LATE?
ZZSSCCH
CH-H-KK

BRMMMM...

SPUT
SPUT
SPUT

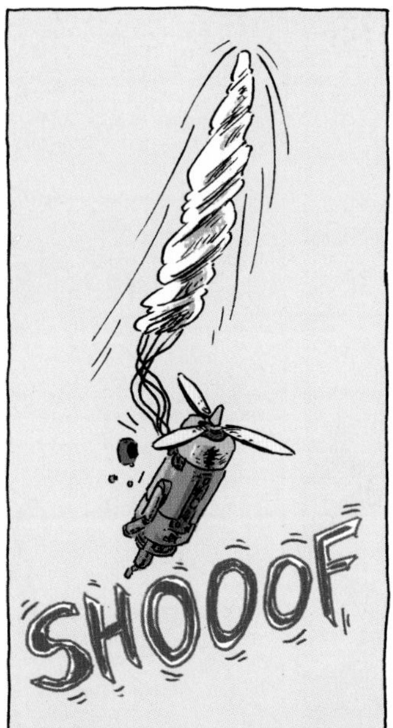
SHOOOF

CR-AA-A-CCCK

OBOY.

HEY, *LILY!*
THAT WAS A *DISASTER!*

COOL CRASH, THOUGH.
NOT A *COMPLETE* DISASTER, ARCHIE.
MY NEW *MARK II* ENGINE WORKED HOW IT'S *SUPPOSED* TO. *KIND OF.*

IT'S MUCH MORE *POWERFUL* THAN THE FIRST ONE.
NICE SAVE WITH THE *TRICKBOX MAGIC!*
YOU ONLY GET *A FEW* OF THOSE IN A LIFETIME, ARCHIE. SAVE 'EM FOR *EMERGENCIES ONLY.*

AND I'VE WORKED ON THIS FOR *TOO LONG NOW* TO LET IT GET *SMASHED TO PIECES.*

VANDALS! *SWINE!*
LOOK WHAT YOU'VE DONE TO *MY LAND!*
UH-OH.
FARMER DUNGWORTH!
YOUR *EXPERIMENTAL AIRCRAFT* SHREDDED HIS TREES.

WHAT ARE YOU, **HOGFORSAKEN WILD BOAR** OR SOMETHING?

Eeeesh.

LET'S EXPLAIN **ANOTHER TIME.**

COME **BACK HERE**, YOU-- YOU...

YOU WICKED, ROTTEN **WARTHOGS!**

Whew
I'M SURE EVEN THE **WARTHOGS** HAVE THEIR OWN **MONSTERS** TO SCARE THEIR KIDS WITH.
HAS ANYONE EVER EVEN **SEEN** A WARTHOG?

DUNNO.
LISTEN, I DON'T WANT TO GET YOU INTO ANY MORE **TROUBLE** TODAY. GO ON, GO HOME.
AW, LILY...

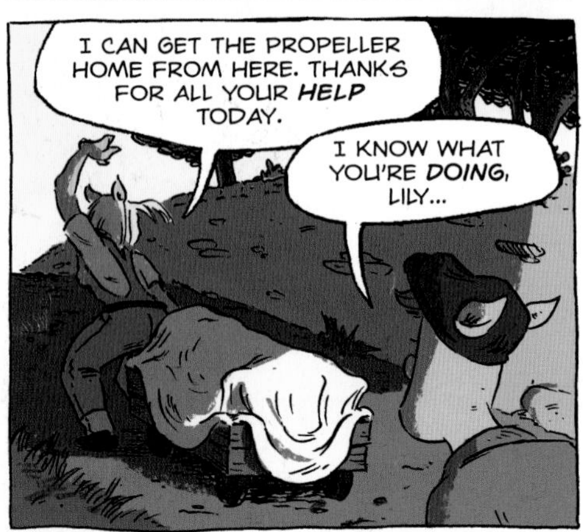
I CAN GET THE PROPELLER HOME FROM HERE. THANKS FOR ALL YOUR **HELP** TODAY.
I KNOW WHAT YOU'RE **DOING**, LILY...

YOU RECKON DUNGWORTH WILL THINK THAT THE **WRECKAGE** OF YOUR AIRCRAFT IS ONE OF **YOUR FATHER'S** FLYING MACHINES...

THAT HE'LL BE ON THE **WARPATH?** MAYBE. I DON'T WANT YOU GETTING **CAUGHT UP** IN THAT.
IF HE TRACKS YOU DOWN, THE **SECRET** WILL BE **OUT**. WITH **YOUR DAD**, I MEAN...?
I'M NOT WORRIED ABOUT THE FARMER. BUT YOU'RE **RIGHT**... I'M GOING TO HAVE TO **TELL** DAD **SOMETIME**.
JUST... **NOT YET**. YOU LET **ME** WORRY ABOUT THAT.
GO **HOME**, ARCHIE. I'LL SEE YOU SOON.

Oh, give me a home
Where the wild boar
roam...

RRRRRRRMMMMMMM

Mmmf

Oh no.
Farmer Dungworth!

Didn't think he'd bother. Not 'til tomorrow, anyway.

...I KNOW YOU'RE A FAMOUS INVENTOR, PROFESSOR FATCHOPS...
AND YOU MAY HAVE THE EAR OF THE PIGMINISTER, BUT IT'S HOGFOLK LIKE ME WHO KEEP THE PIGDOM PLAINS RUNNING.

WE HAVE **A MUTUAL RELIANCE** ON EACH OTHER, DUNGWORTH-- AS IT **SHOULD** BE.

I'M NOT **BLIND** TO THAT.

YET ARE YOU SIGHTLESS WHEN IT COMES TO THE CONCERNS OF **SAFETY**, SIR? OR TO SIMPLE **RESPECT** FOR MY **PROPERTY?**

YOU ARE THE **ONLY INDIVIDUAL** UPON THE PLAINS **CAPABLE** OF CREATING AN INVENTION LIKE THIS.

ACTUALLY, THAT'S NOT QUITE **TRUE**, DUNGWORTH...

DUCKFEED AND SLOPDASH!

DON'T ATTEMPT TO **DELUDE** ME, FATCHOPS! I READ THE **NEWSPAPERS!**

YOU MAKE MACHINES THAT FLY!
MY EXPERIMENTS EXTEND TO SOME SUCCESSFUL HOT-AIR BALLOONING, A BIT OF ROCKETRY, AND SUCHLIKE.
AS YET, I KNOW OF NO INVENTION THAT CAN FLY UNDER ITS OWN POWER AND SUSTAIN IT AT GOOD RATES OF SPEED.
SUCH FANCIES ARE, REGRETTABLY, STILL THE DOMAIN OF MYSTICS AND WITCHES.

AND I AM TELLING YOU THAT THIS THING FLEW. IT WAS A MIGHTY PROJECTILE, A HUGE BULLET WITH WINGS.
AS FAR AS I COULD TELL, IT STAYED ALOFT AND DID NOT DO SO BY MEANS OF MAGIC.

THE TREES WILL RECOVER, BUT IT COULD EASILY HAVE BEEN MUCH WORSE.
I SAW A GIRL AND A BOY THERE. I ASSUMED THEY WERE RESPONSIBLE FOR LAUNCHING THE THING.
Sigh
STEP THIS WAY PLEASE, DUNGWORTH.

I HAVE BUT ONE DAUGHTER, SIR, AND NO SON. SHE IS A CLEVER GIRL AND IS READYING HERSELF TO ATTEND MAESTER CUTHBERT'S COLLEGE NEXT YEAR.
IT IS EASY TO FOLLOW THE LINE OF YOUR THOUGHT--THAT SHE TOOK ONE OF MY TEST VEHICLES AND LAUNCHED IT.

BUT AS YOU CAN SEE, SIR, ALL OF THESE ARE PROTOTYPES...
THOUGH I FEEL MYSELF TO BE CLOSE, NONE OF THESE MACHINES HAVE WORKED... AT LEAST, NOT IN THE WAY YOU DESCRIBE.
HRRRMMPPH.
I AM A SCIENTIST AND ENGINEER... I WILL NOT USE MAGIC TO GET FAST RESULTS. WE MUST SOLVE THE PROBLEMS OF FLIGHT RESPONSIBLY.

HOWEVER... YOU SAID YOU HAVE THE WRECKAGE OF THIS *PROJECTILE* OUTSIDE...?
PERHAPS I CAN HELP *IDENTIFY* IT.

SEE IT FOR YOURSELF... IF IT ISN'T ONE OF YOUR NEFARIOUS DEVICES, THEN WHOSE IS IT?
I HAVE MY SUSPICIONS.

WELL, SIR? YOUR CONSIDERED OPINION?
REMARKABLE. THIS IS QUITE *SOPHISTICATED*...

I HAVE PLAYED WITH *SIMILAR* DESIGNS...
BUT I HAVE NOT *CONSTRUCTED* THEM. THE BUILDER OF THIS CRAFT SEEMS TO HAVE *SOLVED PROBLEMS* THAT I HAVEN'T YET...

OF ALL THE *IRRESPONSIBLE*...
YOU *ADMIRE* IT! YOU ADMIRE THE MAKER OF THE BEASTLY THING!
WELL, IN TERMS OF *PURE ENGINEERING*, IT IS *WORTHY* OF ADMIRATION.

WE SHOULD CALL IN THE AUTHORITIES.
DO. THEY WILL COME STRAIGHT TO *ME* AS AN *EXPERT* TO HELP THEM UNDERSTAND BOTH WHAT AND WHOM THEY ARE *DEALING WITH*.

I CAN ASSURE YOU THAT THIS MATTER NEEDS ***INVESTIGATING.*** I WILL ENDEAVOR TO ***TRACK*** THE ***OWNER*** OF THIS MACHINE.

IN THE INTERESTS OF ***SINCERE NEIGHBORLY CIVILITY***, ISN'T THAT AN ***ENTIRELY REASONABLE*** AND ***EQUITABLE OFFER*** TO MAKE, FARMER DUNGWORTH...?

I HOPE IT WILL ***SATISFY*** YOU. I WILL REPORT MY FINDINGS TO YOU AND ANY ***RELEVANT AUTHORITIES.***
HRRRMPH
PROFESSOR FATCHOPS, I'M A ***PRACTICAL PIG***... A ***HUMBLE FARMER.***
ALTHOUGH I'VE GROWN ***RICH*** FROM THE ***FAT OF THE LAND***, I WORK ***HARD*** FOR A LIVING.

I WILL ADMIT THAT I AM NOT A ***GREATLY LEARNED HOG***, SO FAR BE IT FROM ***ME*** TO THINK THAT ***I*** KNOW HOW HOGKIND SHOULD LIVE.
BUT I KNOW ***THIS MUCH***...

...IF PIGS WERE SUPPOSED TO FLY...
RRRMM

WHAT IN SEVEN SHADES OF SWILL IS *THAT?*

THAT IS THE *WARNING SIREN.*

WARNING SIREN? FOR WHAT?

FOR A *WARTHOG ATTACK.*

WARTHOGS? IT *CAN'T* BE. IT'S BEEN *DECADES...*

LISTEN-- THAT *SOUND,* OVER THE SIREN...

COMING CLOSER...

RRRMMMMM
RRMMMMM

DID YOU SEE THAT THING ON THE UNDERSIDE? THAT FACE?
LISTEN TO ME, DUNGWORTH...

IT'S AN INVASION!
DO AS THE EMERGENCY RULES SAY. GO HOME, HOLE UP. TURN ON YOUR WIRELESS AND FOLLOW THE INSTRUCTIONS YOU HEAR.

YOU SAID NO HOG COULD BUILD A FLYING MACHINE LIKE--
DUNGWORTH...

DID YOU HEAR ME?
GO HOME.
Y-YES, OF COURSE...

DAD...?

LILY...!
INSIDE, QUICKLY!

DAD, WERE THOSE REALLY WARTHOG AIRCRAFT?
ASTRO-BINOCULARS? NO, NOT STRONG ENOUGH. QUICKLY...

...THE OBSERVATORY! MAYBE WE CAN TRACK THEM WITH THE TELESCOPE.
TRACK THEM?

MIGHT NEED THESE, THEN.

CLACK WHRRRRR

CHNNNNG

THEY WERE HEADING DUE EAST, DAD.
MMMM?
YES. YES. THAT'S WHAT I THOUGHT, TOO.

LILY, TAKE THESE BINOCULARS. SCAN THE HORIZON... TO THE NORTH AND WEST.
BUT, DAD, THE WARTHOGS WENT DUE EAST...
WRRRRRRRRR

SCAN THE HORIZON, LILY!
I AM! BUT WHAT AM I LOOKING FOR?

FIRES.

...
NO FIRES.

NO EVIDENCE OF-- OF BOMBARDMENT FROM ABOVE, ANYWHERE.
THANK THE ALLFATHER FOR THAT.

AHA! THERE THEY ARE!
HERE, LOOK...

I SEE THEM!
QUICK, DAD-- TAKE SOME PICTURES WITH THE TELESCOPE CAMERA...
ALREADY DONE.

FEH!... IF ONLY WE COULD CHART THEIR POSITION...

HERE. BROUGHT THE NAVI-CALCULATOR.
GOOD GIRL!

THEY'RE OVER OINKSBURY, HEADING FOR OLD HAMTON PALACE.
BY TROTTSTY'S BEARD! YOU'RE RIGHT.
THEY WERE ALREADY COMING BACK AROUND WHEN THEY FLEW OVER US.

THEY'RE ON A CIRCULAR COURSE...
THEY'RE HEADING BACK TO WHEREVER THEY CAME FROM... OVER THE MOUNTAINS, IN THE WILDBOAR WILDERNESS...
INDEED!

THAT WAS A SCOUTING RUN.
TO CHECK OUT THE PIGDOM... OUR RESOURCES, OUR DEFENSES...

AND PROBABLY TO SEE HOW GOOD THEIR AIRCRAFTS' RANGE IS...
I THINK THEY WANTED TO ANNOUNCE THEIR PRESENCE, TO SCARE US... NOT SPY ON US.
IT WORKED. DID YOU SEE DUNGWORTH?

BUT THREE AIRCRAFT AREN'T EXACTLY AN INVASION FORCE. THEY COULD JUST BE PIRATES.
PERHAPS.

WHATEVER THEY WERE UP TO, WE'RE NOT READY.

DRRRR DRRRR

THE HOTLINE!
THE PIGMINISTER PRIME!
DRRRR

HERCULES FATCHOPS SPEAKING...
YESSIR... HALF THE PIGDOM MUST'VE SEEN THEM. YES, I TRACKED THEIR PROGRESS. MANAGED TO SNAP A COUPLE OF PICTURES.

AN EMERGENCY MEETING? TOMORROW MORNING?
YESSIR. AN EARLY START, SIR.

BUT WE SHOULD REMEMBER THAT THREE AIRCRAFT DON'T CONSTITUTE A WHOLE INVASION FORCE.
NO, SIR. INDEED, SIR. UNTIL TOMORROW, SIR. GOODBYE.

WHY DID I SAY THAT? THE IDEA OF FLYING WARTHOGS IS TERRIFYING! THE WHOLE PIGDOM WILL PANIC...
IT WAS MY FAULT, DAD. I JUST SAID THAT TO MAKE YOU FEEL LESS WORRIED.

I KNOW, LILY. AND IT WASN'T YOUR FAULT...
Sigh

ZZZZZ...
SNFF...
ZZZZ

MARK I...

WHAT'S LEFT OF MY *MARK II*.

I WONDER...

knock knock
KNOCK KNOCK KNOCK
WHAT, *ALREADY?*
!
SASHA...? WHAT ARE YOU DOING HERE AT THIS HOUR?
I HEAR YOU NEED SOME HELP *TIDYING UP.* YOU CAN'T INVITE DECENT PIGFOLK INTO THIS *RAT STY.*
HELLO, *AUNTIE SASHA!* HI, ARCHIE!

THE PIGMINISTER PRIME'S TEAM WILL BE HERE IN ***HALF AN HOUR!***
QUITE SO. GOOD JOB YOUR DAUGHTER CALLED ME IN TO ***HELP***.
ARCHIE, HELP YOUR COUSIN LILY.

OH, ***FARTWEEDS!*** I ALMOST FORGOT!
LILY, CAN YOU HIDE THE ***WRECKAGE*** OF THAT THING DUNGWORTH BROUGHT BY LAST NIGHT...? DON'T WANT THE PIGMINISTER SEEING THAT...

HE MIGHT THINK ***I*** BUILT IT. THIS IS ALL HAPPENING ***TOO QUICKLY!***
YOU ***ALL RIGHT***, DAD?

YES. HURRY UP, PLEASE, YOUNG LADY!
THAT'S A MYSTERY TO BE SOLVED ***ANOTHER DAY***. THINK I ALREADY KNOW THE ***ANSWER*** TO IT, ANYWAY...

THERE WE ARE! MORE **HASTE**, LESS **SPEED.**

WHAT WOULD YOU DO **WITHOUT** ME, DEAR BROTHER?

THEY'RE HERE!

MY GOODNESS! **PIGMINISTER FLANKSFORD**, HERE, IN OUR LITTLE NEIGHBORHOOD!

SOMETIMES I **FORGET** HOW **CLEVER AND FAMOUS** YOU ARE, HERCULES.

Grunt

PERHAPS THE PIGMINISTER PRIME AND HIS ENTOURAGE WOULD LIKE A REFRESHING **CUP OF TEA** AND SOME **CUCUMBER AND RODENT SANDWICHES** FOR **BREAKFAST.**

LET'S TAKE A LOOK AT THIS **KITCHEN**, SHALL WE?

THE WARTHOGS HAVE FLYING MACHINES. AIRCRAFT. HOW DID THEY GET THIS TECHNOLOGY?
HOW FAR OFF ARE WE FROM GETTING SOMETHING SIMILAR LAUNCHED?
A FEW WEEKS... AT BEST, SIR.

IT'S NOT AS SIMPLE AS THAT, SIR. I NEED TIME TO PERFECT MY DESIGNS SO THAT THEY'LL STAY IN THE AIR.
EVEN WITH HELP, I'M WEEKS AWAY FROM GETTING ANYTHING WORKABLE TESTED, LET ALONE LAUNCHED.

YOU HAVE ONE WEEK, FATCHOPS. AND ALL THE RESOURCES YOU NEED.

SIR, I'M NOT SURE YOU'RE LISTENING PROPERLY.

IT'S NOT POSSIBLE.
WHAT ABOUT THAT YOUNG TROTTERS FELLOW-- YOUR PROTÉGÉ? CAN'T HE HELP?

HAM TROTTERS?
PIGMINISTER... DIDN'T YOU KNOW? IT WAS IN ALL THE PAPERS.

HAM TROTTERS WANTED TO USE MAGIC TO HELP KEEP HIS MACHINES IN THE AIR, SO MY BROTHER HERE DISMISSED HIM. WE DON'T EVEN KNOW WHERE HE IS.
OH?

IT'S ABOUT MAKING THE AIRCRAFT ***SAFE***, SIR...

IF YOU USE MAGIC TO KEEP THEM FLYING-- WELL, SPELLS ***FADE***, AND THE MACHINES ***CRASH***.

IT'S ALWAYS BEEN MY AMBITION... MY ***DREAM***... TO INVENT AN AIRCRAFT THAT WILL STAY ALOFT UNDER ***ITS OWN POWER***.

WHY DON'T YOU TELL THEM ABOUT YOUR *MARK I PROTOTYPE?* IT'S *TESTED.* IT'S *A WORKING AIRCRAFT READY TO GO.*

ARE YOU *NUTS?* IF I *EMBARRASSED* HIM IN FRONT OF *THIS CROWD*, MY DAD WOULD *SKIN ME ALIVE!*

...IT'S NOT JUST ABOUT THE *POWER* OF THE ENGINE. IT'S ABOUT THE *CONTROL MECHANISMS*, THE *RUDDER*, THE *WING SHAPE*...

YOU WILL SOLVE THESE PROBLEMS IN *SHORT ORDER*, HERCULES.

ANOTHER SIGHTING RUN. BUT IN BROAD DAYLIGHT THIS TIME.
THEY'RE MAPPING THE PIGDOM PLAINS.
NOT AS YET, SIR.

THEY'RE VIOLATING OUR SKIES. HOW FAR BEHIND CAN A LAND INVASION BE?
WE MUST PREPARE-- AND WE CLEARLY HAVE ONLY A VERY SHORT TIME TO READY OURSELVES.

OUR AERIAL DEFENSE IS IN YOUR HANDS NOW, FATCHOPS!
REMEMBER-- ONE WEEK! TIME IS OF THE ESSENCE!

DELICIOUS SANDWICHES, BY THE WAY, MS....?
MRS. SASHA WIGGSLY, HERCULES'S SISTER. THANK YOU, SIR.

YOU. WHAT'S YOUR NAME?
S-SLUDGEWELL, SIR.
SLUDGEWELL, EH...?

SLUDGEWELL, YOU STAY HERE AND HELP PROFESSOR FATCHOPS. YOU'RE OUR LIAISON. SEE THAT HE GETS WHATEVER HE NEEDS.
Y-YESSIR!
Sigh

VROOM

LILY...?
WOW.

YOU WERE WAY AHEAD OF ME. YOU'VE ALREADY MADE THE MODIFICATIONS!
AH, ARCHIE. YEAH, I DID IT LAST NIGHT.
I'M GLAD YOU'RE HERE. YOU CAN CHECK THAT THE COAST IS CLEAR FOR ME TO TAKE OFF.

TAKE OFF? NO TEST RUN FIRST?
NO TIME.
THOSE WARTHOG CRAFT WERE SPOTTED OVER SWILLINGTON. I MIGHT BE ABLE TO FOLLOW THEM IF I HURRY. SEE WHERE THEY'RE GOING.

OUR PROBLEM IS A LACK OF INFORMATION. MAKES SENSE TO DO A SCOUTING RUN OF OUR OWN.
B-BUT WON'T YOUR DAD HEAR?

I'M GOING OUT THE BACK ROUTE, VIA THE SOUTHERN FIELD. WIND'S PERFECT. SHOULD MUFFLE ANY NOISE.
CLOSE UP FOR ME, WILL YOU?
UH...OF COURSE!

DON'T WORRY, ARCHIE. WE'VE DONE THIS A HUNDRED TIMES. LIKE YOU SAID, WE KNOW IT ALL WORKS...
THIS TIME I'M JUST GOING A BIT FARTHER THAN USUAL.
But you're chasing warthogs...

YEAH. I WANT TO GET A CLOSER LOOK AT SOME OF THEIR MACHINES!
YOU SURE MADE A LOT OF IMPROVEMENTS. WHAT'S THAT THING?

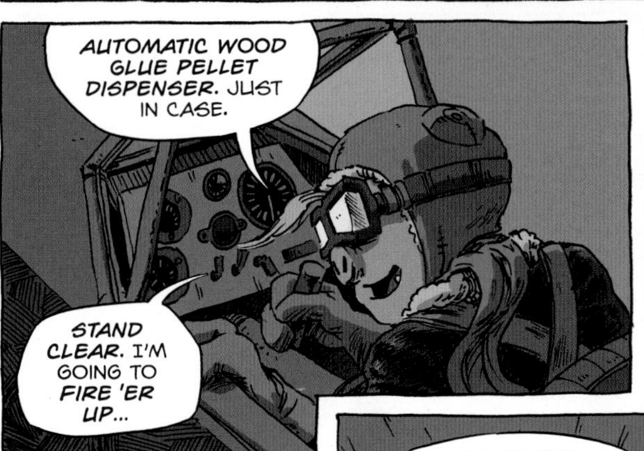
AUTOMATIC WOOD GLUE PELLET DISPENSER. JUST IN CASE.
STAND CLEAR. I'M GOING TO FIRE 'ER UP...

I SURE HOPE YOU KNOW WHAT YOU'RE DOING, LILY.

CHK...
BBROOOOOM

ARCHIE, I'VE NEVER BEEN MORE CERTAIN OF ANYTHING IN MY LIFE.

LILY, WAIT!

YOU FORGOT YOUR TRICKBOX...

MAY THE *AERIAL PIG* WATCH OVER YOU...

Won't say *no* to a bit of *good luck*, though...

IS LUCK MAGIC?
IF I WISH FOR THE BLESSING OF THE GREAT WINGED ONE...

...FOR THE PROTECTION OF THE AERIAL PIG...

IF THAT HELPS ME GET THIS THING ALOFT...

RRRRRRRMMM

...IS THAT BAD?

O ALLFATHER SKYPIG THE SKY, HIS STY GIVE US WINGS SO THERE WE MIGHT FLY...

IN THE HEAVENLY BARNYARD YOUR WHIMS WE TEND FROM THE PLAINS, SKYWARD OUR WAY WE WEND...

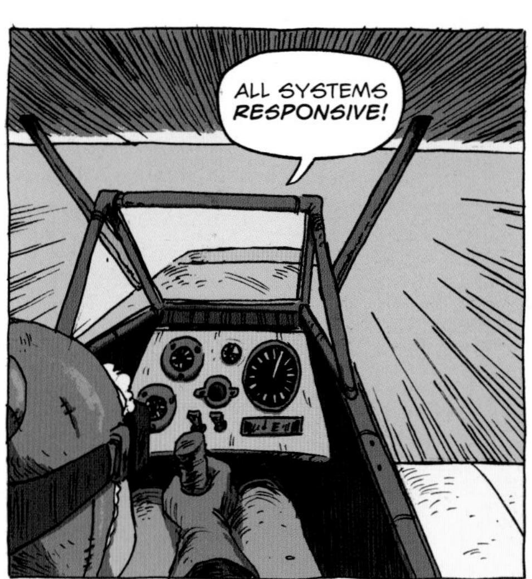
ALL SYSTEMS
RESPONSIVE!

Oh,
bunnies!
I'M
ON MY
WAY.

SWILLINGTON...

A-HA.

LOOKS LIKE SOME KIND OF A RAID...

RRRRRRRROOOOWWMMMM

THE WARTHOGS ARE STEALING STUFF!

WHOA!
ZORCH
ZORCH

HOLY CATS!
NEGATIVE ENERGY...THAT'S NON-CARDINAL MAGIC!
THOSE PITCHFORK THINGS-- SOME SORT OF ANTI-TRICKBOXES...?

WHAAAA!
FRAZAAAAP

Courage, Lily...
THAT'S IT! G'WAN, SCOOT!

DIDN'T EXPECT US TO HAVE OUR OWN FLYING MACHINES, DIDJA?

YEAH, GO ON! GET LOST!

Oh...

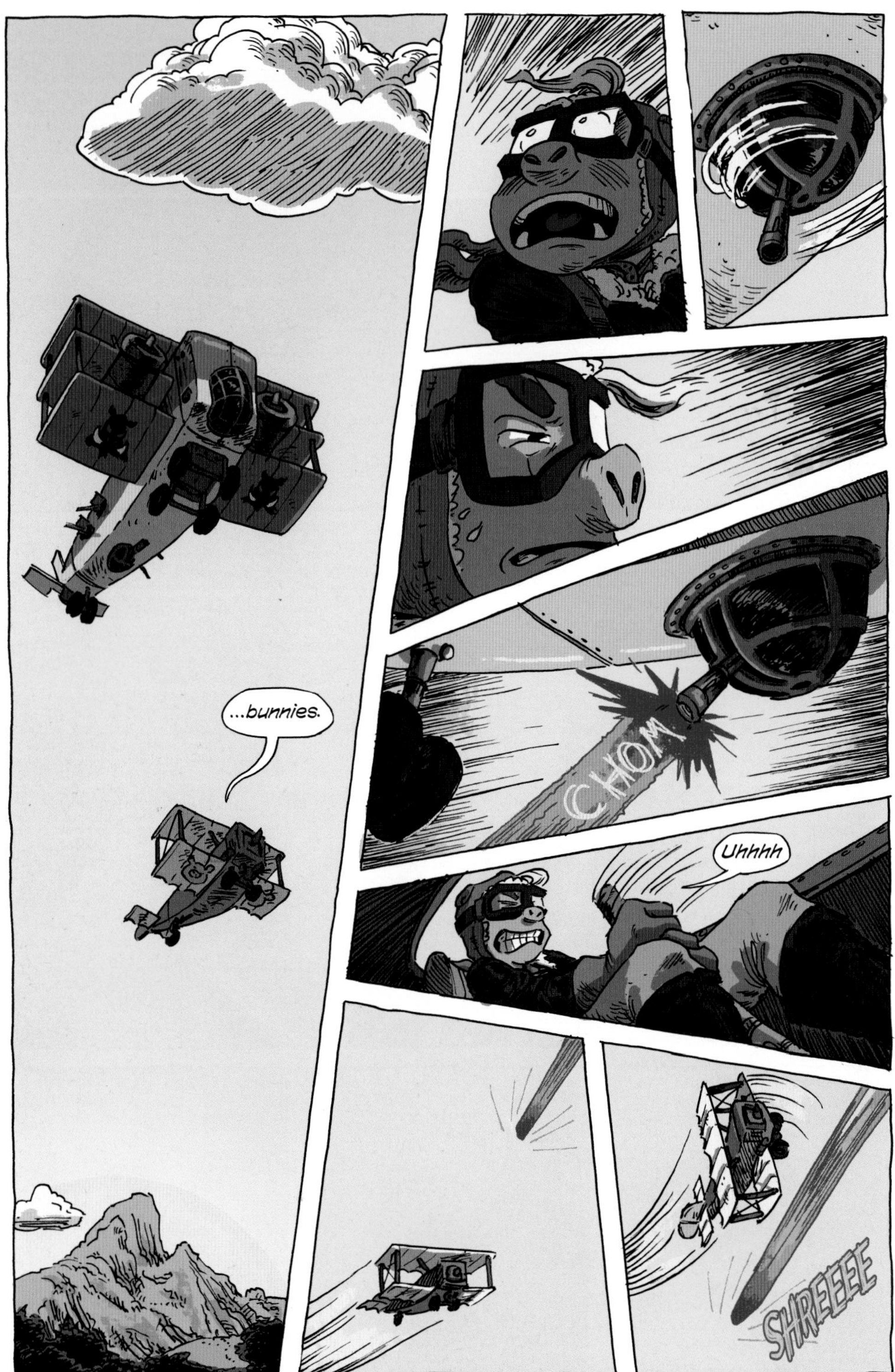

...bunnies.
CHOM
Uhhhh
SHREEEE

CHOM
CHOM
CHOM
ZORCH
ZORCH
OKAY.
SO YOU DON'T WANT TO PLAY *NICELY*.
CHK
CHOK
CHOK
CHOK
CHOK
CHOK

OKAY, **OKAY**...

YOU WANT SOME, TOO...?

CHOK
CHOK
CHOK

WHOO-
HOOO!
PERCY! LOOK!
COULD IT BE...ONE OF OURS?
WHATEVER IT IS, IT'S GOT 'EM ON THE RUN!
WHOEVER YOU ARE... THANK YOU! MAY THE GREAT WINGED ONE BLESS YA!
SPLITCH
SPLOTCH
CHOK
CHOK
CHOK
CHOK
CHOK
SWIIP
CHOM

FRAZAAP
CORKS! OUR LITTLE ANGEL'S TAKEN A HIT!
OH NO!
WAIT-- NO, HE'S OKAY... HE'S GOING AFTER THEM AGAIN!
HE'S MORE MANEUVERABLE THAN THOSE WARTHOGS...
...AND IT LOOKS LIKE HE'S DONE THEM SOME REAL DAMAGE!
WHO IS THAT UP THERE?
Oh no. FUEL'S LOW.
IF I'M GOING TO MAKE IT HOME, I HAVE TO TURN BACK NOW.
KEEP ME SAFE, O WINGED ONE...

KARUMPHH

Price: 2½ PP

Hamday, Hogtween 11th, 1101

The Pigdom Plains Post

MYSTERIOUS AERIAL HOG BRINGS DOWN WARTHOG FLYING MACHINE

An artist's impression based on descriptions by our on-site witnesses to THE BATTLE of SWILLINGTON, **Corky Spamdoyle** and **Percy Heffingt**... workers for Swillington Farmhouse Industries. See full report, beginnin...

Percy Heffington: "The Warthogs landed – terrifying they were, slavering, hairy great barbarians with giant tusks. They had magic weapons – you could hear the crackle of bad energy. They promised to shoot us there on the spot if we didn't give them what they wanted."

Corky Spamdoyle: "They took off, into the air – and suddenly, he came out of nowhere. Like a little mosquito buzzing angrily around some big flying alligators, he was. He looked little, but he wasn't to be messed with!"

EYEWITNESS ACCOUNTS on Page 2

The WARTHOGS – What is Known

By our History Correspondent, Natasha Svinya

We here in the Pigdom Plains have always known that others live in the realms beyond the safe walls of the mountain ranges that surround us. We pride ourselves on our relations with the residents of the many island nations in the Pearly Sea, with whom we have shared trade relations as far back as records go...

Is this a first ... INVASION of ou... Pigdom by Wart...

By our roving corre... Patrick Hamkins

Yesterday a raiding party in three Warthog flying machines landed in Swillington. They threatened workers at Swillington Farmhouse Industries' main warehouse, stole goods worth over ten thousand Pigdom groats, mostly grain and preserved foods, but also a year's supply of fuel and some portable miniature steam engines. These were designed by the esteemed Professor Hercules Fatchops, inventor of the Pigdom's Commercial Trackway system and many other household innovations. Professor Fatchops is known to be working on flying machines

(continued in page 4)

"...THE CREW OF THE DOWNED WARTHOG AIRCRAFT ESCAPED BEFORE PIGDOM AUTHORITIES COULD REACH IT. THEY WERE TRACKED TO A PASS OVER THE WARTHOG MOUNTAINS, EVIDENTLY MAKING FOR THEIR OWN TERRITORY..."
IDIOTS! THEY LET THE CREW ESCAPE? THEY'D HAVE TOLD US EVERYTHING WE NEED TO KNOW...
PSHAW!

AS FOR THIS MYSTERIOUS "AERIAL HOG"...
HE BROUGHT THAT WARTHOG MACHINE DOWN AND CHASED THE OTHERS AWAY.
YOU'RE JUST ANGRY BECAUSE SOMEHOG GOT AIRBORNE BEFORE YOU.

YES! YES, I AM!
IF THAT IDIOT FLANKSFORD HADN'T HAD ME DIGGING TUNNELS, I'D HAVE FINISHED A PROTOTYPE AIRCRAFT YEARS AGO!
DAD... I COULD HELP.

YOU CAN INVENT A WHOLE NEW WORLD...TRACKWAYS, TRAMS, ENGINES, COMMUNICATIONS, AND WHAT THANKS D'YOU GET?
"WE NEED A FLYING MACHINE IN A WEEK." ONE WEEK!
IDIOTS!

DAD, LET ME HELP YOU!
NO, LILY.
DON'T WANT YOU INVOLVED WITH THESE IMBECILIC GOVERNMENT TYPES...

BUT I'D BE HELPING YOU. I'M NOT A PIGLET ANYMORE, DAD.

I SAID **NO!**

HELLO! FRONT DOOR WAS ***OPEN***, SO I LET MYSELF IN.
BETTER NOT LEAVE IT ***UNLOCKED*** IF THERE'S A WARTHOG INVASION, EH? ***HAHAHA!***

UM, GOOD MORNING, ***MR. SLUDGEWELL.***
ARCHIE, GET MR. SLUDGEWELL SOME ***TEA***, WILL YOU?
PROFESSOR FATCHOPS, THE DOWNED WARTHOG CRAFT IS BEING BROUGHT HERE TODAY AS PER YOUR INSTRUCTIONS.

YES, **GOOD.** LET'S SEE WHAT WE CAN ***LEARN*** FROM IT...
EXCUSE ME A MOMENT...

Mmphh

NNngh

LILY...?
Oh... HELLO, AUNTIE SASHA.

LILY, DARLING... ARE YOU ALL RIGHT?
YEAH.

SOMETIMES YOUR FATHER'S LIKE A **BEAR** WITH A **SORE HEAD**.

HE'S A **BOOR**. AN OLD **WART-HOG!**
HE CAN BE A BIT **BRUSQUE** WHEN HE'S UNDER **PRESSURE**, I GRANT YOU.

WELL, NOW... WHAT'S **THIS** THAT YOU'VE THROWN AWAY?

A **FOCUSING TALISMAN!** DIDN'T YOUR **FATHER** GIVE YOU THIS?
YEAH...

NOT LIKE HE **BELIEVES** IN IT, THOUGH.
SCIENCE AND **BELIEF** AREN'T AS **MUTUALLY EXCLUSIVE** IN YOUR FATHER'S MIND AS HE'D LIKE FOLKS TO **THINK**...

AFTER ALL, HE GREW UP WITH **ME.**
THERE'S A **REASON** WHY HE GAVE YOU THIS...

THOSE TALISMANS ARE JUST FOR LUCK. **KEEPSAFES.**
MAYBE... BUT A BIT OF BELIEF IN **GOOD LUCK** NEVER HURT ANYHOG.

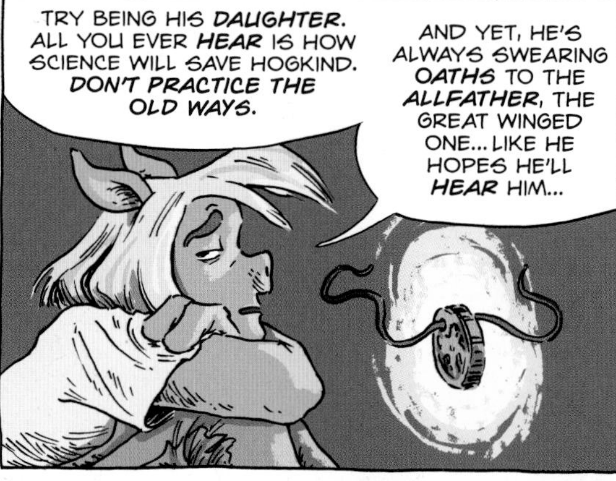
TRY BEING HIS **DAUGHTER.** ALL YOU EVER **HEAR** IS HOW SCIENCE WILL SAVE HOGKIND. **DON'T PRACTICE THE OLD WAYS.**
AND YET, HE'S ALWAYS SWEARING **OATHS** TO THE **ALLFATHER**, THE GREAT WINGED ONE... LIKE HE HOPES HE'LL **HEAR** HIM...

IT'S THE **IDEA** OF **BEING HEARD** THAT'S **IMPORTANT**.

HE DOESN'T LISTEN TO **ME.** HE CAN BE SO SWINEHEADED AND **MEAN** SOMETIMES.
I JUST WANT TO HELP. HE DOESN'T KNOW HOW MUCH **I KNOW.**
I THINK HE **DOES**...

...HE JUST DOESN'T WANT YOU FALLING INTO THE SAME TRAP HE DID, WORKING FOR ALL THOSE FAT-BOTTOMED, SELF-IMPORTANT FOOLS...
HE WANTS SOMETHING BETTER FOR YOU.

IT MIGHT SOUND CORNY, LILY, BUT YOU ARE WHAT HE BELIEVES IN.
FUNNY WAY OF SHOWING IT.

AND WHAT ABOUT YOU, LILY LEANCHOPS? WHAT DO YOU BELIEVE? DO YOU STILL HAVE THAT TRICKBOX I GAVE YOU?

OF COURSE! I WOULDN'T PART WITH THAT FOR ANYTHING!

THAT'S NICE TO KNOW. THAT'S MY KEEPSAFE TO YOU. YOU KNOW HOW MUCH I LOVE YOU, LILY. I DON'T WANT ANYTHING EVER TO HAPPEN TO YOU.

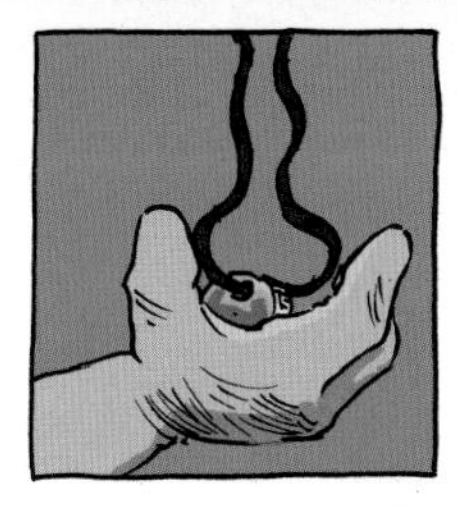

Oh, AUNTIE SASHA... WHAT WOULD I DO WITHOUT YOU?

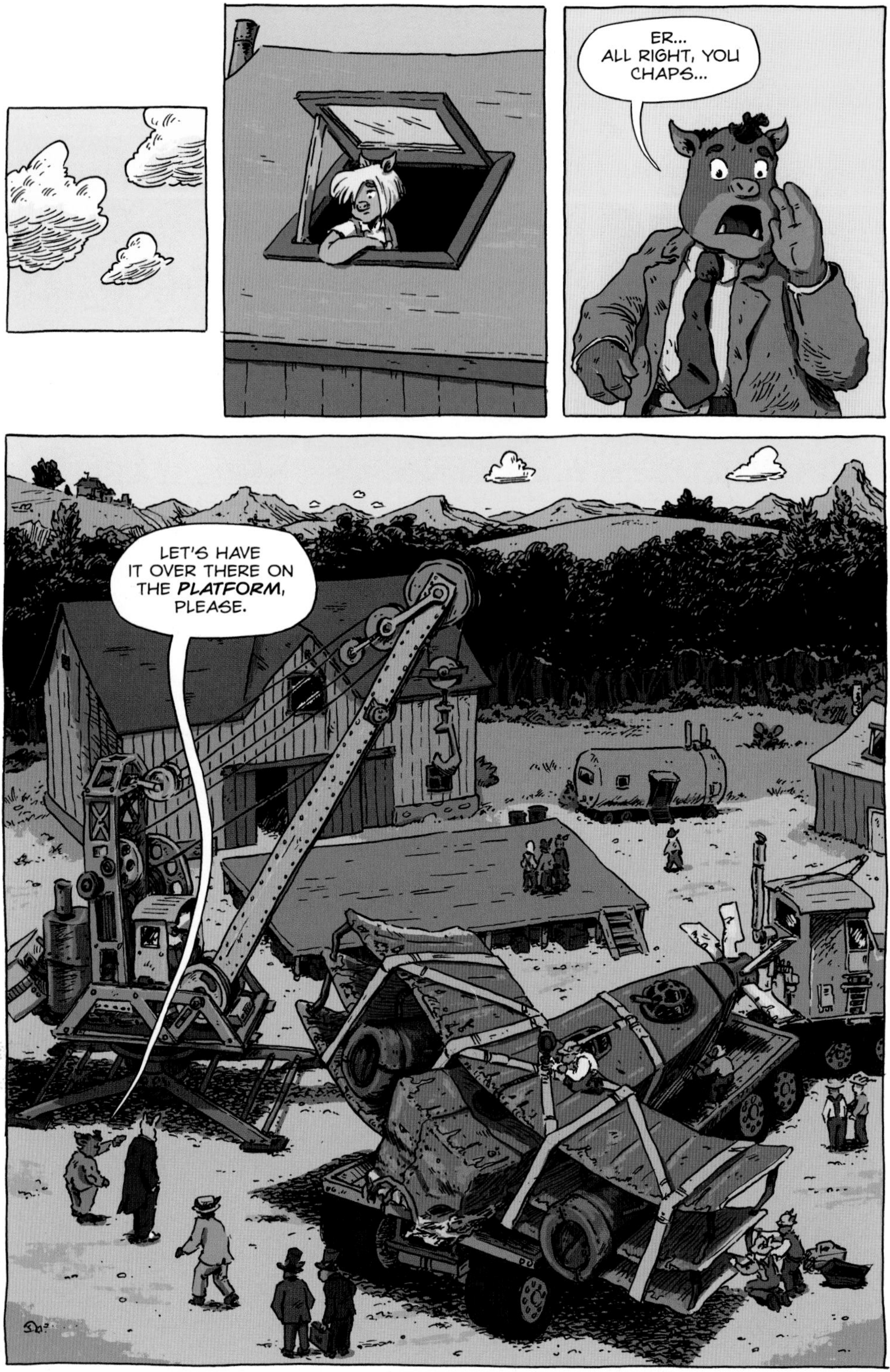

ER...
ALL RIGHT, YOU CHAPS...

LET'S HAVE IT OVER THERE ON THE *PLATFORM*, PLEASE.

THERE'S NO WAY THAT THING COULD **EVER** FLY.
WELL, **NO.** THAT **AERIAL HONKER** SHOT IT DOWN **GOOD AND PROPER**, DIDN'T HE?

THAT'S NOT WHAT I MEAN.
"AERIAL HONKER"? IS THAT WHAT YOU'RE CALLING THE ***ANGEL OF SWILLINGTON?***
ANGEL OF SWILLINGTON?

I COINED THAT NAME FOR THE MYSTERIOUS PIGDOM AIRCRAFT THAT SAW OFF THE WARTHOGS. BUT I ***LIKE AERIAL HONKER*** BETTER!
I ***KNOW*** YOU FROM SOMEWHERE, DON'T I?

PATRICK HAMKINS, REPORTER FROM ***THE PIGDOM POST.***
PROFESSOR FATCHOPS, I'M A ***GREAT ADMIRER*** OF YOUR WORK...

Ah. WE ***HAVE*** MET BEFORE.
MR. HAMKINS, I'M AFRAID OUR WORK HERE IS ***TOP SECRET.*** THERE'S A ***NEWS BLACKOUT*** IN EFFECT... PIGMINISTER PRIME'S ***ORDERS.***

WWWRRUNCH

MR. HAMKINS, I'M ***SORRY***, BUT I'M GOING TO HAVE TO ASK YOU TO ***LEAVE.***

WHAT? YOU CAN'T DO THAT! THE CITIZENS OF THE PIGDOM HAVE A RIGHT TO KNOW--
SECRECY IS OF THE UTMOST IMPORTANCE. THE PIGDOM MAY BE AT WAR. AND WE DON'T REALLY YET KNOW THE TRUE NATURE OF OUR ENEMY...

THIS IS OUTRAGEOUS.
BE THAT AS IT MAY, MR. HAMKINS. IT'S BEEN DECIDED.

MAY I DIRECT YOU TO OUR PRESS OFFICE? I'LL MAKE SURE THAT YOU ARE THE FIRST OF OUR CORRESPONDENTS TO BE INFORMED OF ANY DEVELOPMENTS...
I'LL GET THE SCOOP? YOU GUARANTEE IT?

THANKS.
NOT AT ALL. SHALL WE CARRY ON?

THERE'S NO WAY THAT THING COULD EVER HAVE FLOWN.
NO?

NOT WITHOUT THE HELP OF SOME SERIOUS MAGIC. AND THOSE WARTHOGS DEFINITELY HAD SOME SERIOUS MAGIC...
YEAH.

ONLY, I NEVER EVER SAW ANYONE STRONG ENOUGH TO SHOOT BOLTS OF MAGIC FROM PITCHFORKS BEFORE.

THEY USED MAGIC TO KEEP THEIR MACHINES IN THE AIR.

MOM SHOWS ME STUFF THE SAME WAY YOUR DAD TEACHES YOU!
...you don't say!

PLUS WE COULD GIVE YOU SOME EXTRA GOOD LUCK SHIELDING.
ARCHIE, NO!

THIS IS JUST A PROTECTION SPELL, LILY.
IT HAS TO STAY UP THERE BECAUSE IT'S COMPLYING WITH THE LAWS OF PHYSICS, NOT THE LAWS OF MAGIC...

MAYBE YOU CAN'T USE MAGIC TO KEEP AN AIRCRAFT IN THE AIR, BUT THERE'S NO REASON WHY YOU CAN'T USE MAGIC TO HELP MAKE THE AIRCRAFT.

OR PROTECT IT!
YOU HAVE TO LET ME LOOK AFTER YOU. IF ANYTHING EVER HAPPENED TO YOU, I'D NEVER FORGIVE MYSELF.
ALL RIGHT.

TELL ME WHAT YOU NEED. WANT A BIGGER FUEL TANK FOR GREATER RANGE? LET'S DO IT.

AND LET'S NAME HER, TOO!

Wingday 12th Hogtween, 1101 YH

The past few days have been both intolerable and intoxicating. I felt overcome by a deep despair in confronting the apparent impossibility of the task I've been given.

And yet, by drawing on all my past ideas and designs, we are shaping the possibility of building something that might actually prove to be serviceable. There is something in the air, a sense of timing and possibility that is helping make this venture cohere.

One thing really bothers me-- the mysterious Angel of Swillington, as Patrick Hamkins dubbed it. Hamkins is a swine and a hack, but his snout for a good story is not in doubt. Perhaps he suspects that I fear that this "Aerial Hog" may prove to be my ex-apprentice, Ham Trotters, but there is nothing I can find in the reports of the craft's appearance that point to Trotters's trademark laziness of design.

MR. SLUDGEWELL, SIR!

MMMRRRM
MMRRRRR

I SET UP THE **CAMOUFLAGE.** YOU'VE GOT A ROUTE STRAIGHT THROUGH TO THE SOUTHERN FIELD.
THE **SOUND-DAMPENING** SPELL WILL KICK IN ON **TAKE-OFF** AND **LANDING.** ANYWAY, THEY'LL **NEVER HEAR** OVER THE **CLATTER** OF THE WORKYARD!

MMMRRRRR

RRRRRR

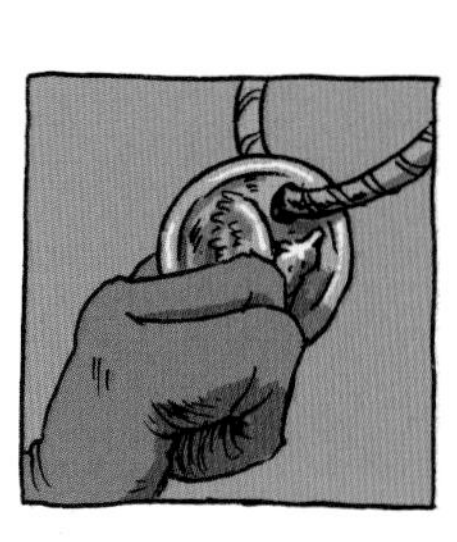

ESMERALD

PIGGLESWICK'S **CLOSE**... NOT HALF AN HOUR AWAY. ***WHY*** PIGGLESWICK? WHAT'S THERE?
...NOT MUCH.

EXCEPT--
ON **MARKET DAY**...
...WHICH IS...

"...TODAY!"
RRMMMMMM

RRMMMM
EMMA'S
RUN FOR YOUR LIVES!
WARTHOGS!

¡¡¡¡¡¡¡OOOOOO

WRRMM

OOOOOOO

CRNCH
MNCH
CRAK
PR-A-AK

OOOOOOO

LOOK!

YES... THERE!
IT'S...
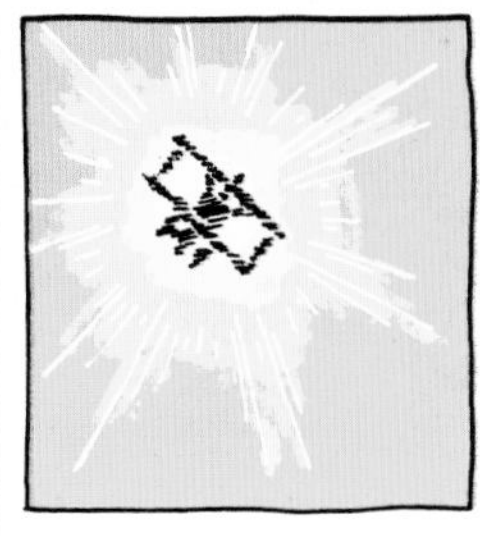

YES!
IT'S THE "AERIAL HONKER"!
I HEARD ABOUT HIM ON THE WIRELESS!
HE'S COME TO SAVE US FROM THOSE MONSTROUS THINGS!
CHOK
CHOK
CHOK
CHOM
CHOM
CHOM
CHOM
RRMMMMMM
PWIIING
ZORCH
ZORCH
THANKS, ARCHIE!
NOW LET'S SEE IF THEY CAN TAKE SOME OF THEIR OWN MEDICINE.

PCHOOO

OOOOOOOOOOOOoooo

KRZONK

HOW'D YOU LIKE *THAT...?*

COURTESY OF MY OWN PERSONAL ***LITTLE MAGIC HELPER!***

AH, DON'T ***LIKE IT***, EH?

YOU'RE NOT GOING TO GET AWAY SO ***EASILY*** THIS TIME.

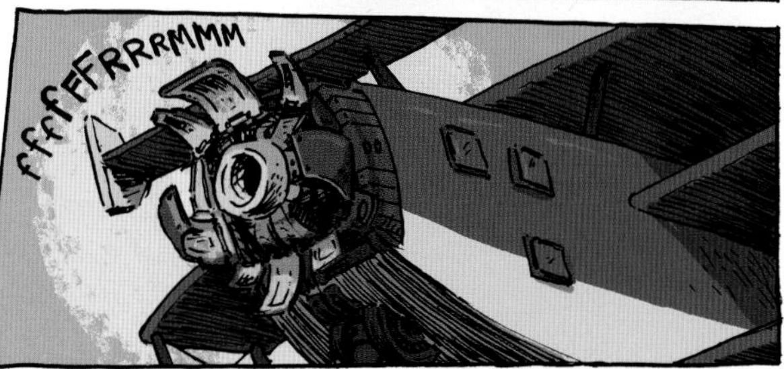

FRROOOOOM

C'MON, ESMERALDA... UP...
UP, OUT OF THIS BARRAGE.
Not fair.

AN ACCELERATION SPELL WRAPPED AROUND AN ENGINE. MAGIC SPEED. I'LL NEVER CATCH UP TO THEM NOW.
THINK, LILY...

THEY'RE HEADING FOR THE LOWEST PEAKS OF THE MOUNTAIN RANGE.
IF I CAN GAIN ENOUGH ALTITUDE, MAYBE I CAN SEE WHERE THEY'RE GOING...

C'MON, ESMERALDA... GIVE ME EVERYTHING YOU'VE GOT!

YEAH, THAT ENGINE WASH IS LIKE A FLARE...

SO THAT'S WHERE THEY'RE GOING.

HERCULES, YOU NEED TO TAKE A BREAK.
MMMM?

NO TIME.
WELL, AT LEAST EAT SOMETHING... I BROUGHT YOU A SANDWICH.

SASHA, PLEASE. I CAME UP HERE TO GET AWAY FROM ALL THOSE IDIOTS IN THE YARD. I NEED SPACE TO THINK...

HERCULES. EAT. OR YOU'LL CRASH.

Munch

WHAT...
IS THAT?
WELCOME HOME, AERIAL HONKER!
ESMERALDA
RRRMMM

SUCCESS?
SORT OF. LET ME PARK ESMERALDA AND I'LL TELL YOU...
ESMERALDA

...EVERYTHING...

SO... WELCOME HOME...
..."AERIAL HONKER."
DAD!
I-I CAN EXPLAIN EVERYTHING...

EXPLAIN? EXPLAIN WHAT, PRECISELY?
EXPLAIN THAT YOU'VE TAKEN A NATIONAL EMERGENCY INTO YOUR OWN HANDS?

I only wanted to help...

EXPLAIN HOW YOU'RE HELPING. EXPLAIN WHY YOU'VE BEEN SHOOTING DOWN WARTHOGS, POSSIBLY MAKING AN ALREADY TENSE SITUATION WORSE...?
EXPLAIN WHY YOU PUT YOURSELF IN SUCH DANGER?

EXPLAIN WHY YOU DIDN'T TELL ME YOU ALREADY HAD A WORKING AIRCRAFT, WHEN I'VE BEEN OUT THERE KNOCKING HEADS WITH IDIOTS TRYING TO CREATE ONE INSIDE OF A WEEK...?
ARE YOU TRYING TO MAKE A FOOL OUT OF ME?
NO, DAD, NO!

THEN PERHAPS YOU'D LIKE TO EXPLAIN HOW YOU DESIGNED AND BUILT...

BWZOOoooNG
...THAT?!

OH, NO, NO-- DON'T TELL ME YOU USED MAGIC! NOT AFTER EVERYTHING I'VE TAUGHT YOU...
OF COURSE NOT! THAT'S JUST A PROTECTION SPELL.
HERCULES, I'M SURE LILY DIDN'T--

PLEASE, SASHA, DON'T INTERRUPT. I WANT TO HEAR WHAT LILY'S GOT TO SAY FOR HERSELF.
I--

THERE I WAS, WORRYING THAT HAM TROTTERS HAD SOLVED ALL THE PROBLEMS OF FLIGHT. BUT I NEEDN'T HAVE WORRIED, BECAUSE MY OWN DAUGHTER DID IT-- AND THEN DIDN'T TELL ME!
NOT ONLY THAT, BUT SHE WENT AGAINST THE MOST IMPORTANT PHILOSOPHICAL ARGUMENT I'VE EVER MADE...
SHE USED MAGIC IN ITS CREATION!

DAD, YOU'RE NOT LISTENING...
DOES IT MATTER IF I'M LISTENING OR NOT? YOU'LL JUST CARRY ON REGARDLESS...

THE VESSEL IS AIRWORTHY UNDER ITS OWN POWER. I BUILT IT MYSELF-- NO MAGIC, NO SPELLS, NO ENCHANTMENTS.
ALL IT HAS IS A PROTECTION SPELL BY ARCHIE AS A DEFENSE AGAINST WARTHOG MISSILES.

WELL...THAT, AND THE SOUND-DAMPENING CHARM...
WHAT?!

ARCHIE IS INVOLVED? OF ALL THE IRRESPONSIBLE...
HERCULES...

SASHA, DON'T INTERFERE. YOU CAN DEAL WITH YOUR BOY HOW YOU SEE FIT.
DAD, ARCHIE DIDN'T--

ENOUGH!

YOU'RE GROUNDED, YOUNG LADY!
DON'T YOU EVEN WANT TO KNOW WHAT I FOUND OUT ABOUT THE WARTHOGS?

YOU HAVE NO PART IN THE MANAGEMENT OF THIS CRISIS.
GO TO YOUR ROOM. I WILL BE UP THERE SHORTLY AND YOU WILL SURRENDER THE KEY TO ME.
YOU'RE GOING TO LOCK ME IN...?!

YES. I ALSO REQUIRE YOUR TALISMAN. I'M CONFISCATING IT.
SERIOUSLY?
HERCULES!

I'll go after her, make sure she's all right.
YOU WILL NOT.
HERCULES! DON'T YOU DARE TELL MY SON WHAT TO DO!

ARCHIE, GO.
I KNOW MY DAUGHTER. SHE WON'T GO ANYWHERE WITHOUT THIS.

WELL, I HOPE YOU'RE HAPPY NOW.
MADE YOUR POINT, DIDN'T YOU? WITH ALL THE TACT OF-- OF A WARTHOG!
SHE BROKE MY TRUST. SHE NEEDS TO LEARN A LESSON.

HERCULES...
I THINK IT'S TIME YOU REALIZED THAT YOUR LITTLE GIRL ISN'T A PIGLET ANYMORE.

MAYBE SHE DIDN'T GO ABOUT THINGS THE WAY SHE SHOULD HAVE, BUT--
SHE NEEDS TO BE PUNISHED.

OH, DON'T BE SUCH A BOOR, HERCULES. AT LEAST HALF THE PROBLEM HERE IS YOU. YOU WILL NOT LISTEN!
SHE'S BEEN TRYING TO GET YOUR ATTENTION FOR YEARS.

CAN'T YOU SEE WHAT AN AMAZING YOUNG LADY SHE IS BECOMING?
MORE SO THAN EVER, IN LIGHT OF THIS REVELATION.

YOU SHOULD BE VERY PROUD OF HER.

NO ADMITTANCE

LILY

WHAT D'YOU THINK YOU'RE DOING?
I WANT TO TALK TO MY DAUGHTER.

LILY...
GO AWAY!
POK

NOT SURPRISING REALLY, EH? NOT AFTER EVERYTHING YOU SAID EARLIER.

HERE. ISN'T THIS WHAT YOU CAME FOR? SHE'S LOCKED IN, DON'T WORRY.
NO, I...

YOU NEED TO GIVE HER TIME...
LOOK, SASHA...
SHE'S PUT ME IN A VERY DIFFICULT POSITION...

OH, WHAT ARE YOU COMPLAINING ABOUT? SHE'S GIVEN YOU EXACTLY WHAT YOU NEEDED.
YOU WANTED A WORKING AIRCRAFT. YOU'VE GOT ONE.

SHE SAID TO GIVE YOU THESE.

NOW IT'S UP TO YOU WHETHER YOU PASS IT OFF AS YOUR OWN OR YOUR DAUGHTER'S WORK.

PROFESSOR FATCHOPS!
WHA--

APOLOGIES FOR WAKING YOU. GRUNTSBY, THE YARD FOREMAN ASKED FOR US... HE'S GOT SOMETHING HE SAYS WE NEED TO SEE...
MMMM?

RIGHT-O.
TELL 'M I'LL BE THERE IN A JIFFY...

LILY?

LILY! I READ YOUR PLANS! YOU'RE A GENIUS!
LILY? ARE YOU AWAKE?
LILY

LILY?

OH NO.

NOT ***EVERYTHING***, NO. I WISH I HAD MY ***TALISMAN***...

I'M TAKING THE ***TRICKBOX*** INSTEAD. Y'KNOW, FOR ***EMERGENCIES***...

LILY, ***I*** HAVE A TALISMAN, TOO...

I WANT YOU TO HAVE IT.

THANK YOU, ARCHIE, BUT **NO.** I CAN'T TAKE THAT FROM YOU.

BESIDES, IF I DON'T HAVE MY TALISMAN, AT LEAST IT'LL ***PROVE TO DAD*** THAT I ***BELIEVED ENOUGH IN SCIENCE*** TO GET ME ***AIRBORNE!***
BRRRRRMmmm

LET'S GO, ESMERALDA!
GO, GO, **GO,** AERIAL HONKER!

GANGWAY!
COMING THROUGH!

I SAY... PROFESSOR FATCHOPS!
NOT NOW, SLUDGEWELL!

LILY...!

ESMERALDA

LILY!
LILY, **NO...** =GASP=
I NEED YOUR **HELP...** =GASP=
...TO **INTERPRET** THE **PLANS...** =GASP=

NOW, **LOOK HERE,** PROFESSOR FATCHOPS...
I REALLY THINK YOU NEED TO **SEE THIS...** AND **EXPLAIN** WHAT'S GOING ON.

I SAY, WHAT IS THIS PLACE? IS IT...
LET ME SEE THAT!

The Pigdom Plains Post

AERIAL HONKER
THE ANGEL OF SWILLINGTON AND PIGGLESWICK
IS A SLIP OF A GIRL
and she is Hercules Fatchops's daughter!
I saw her secret workshop
By our roving correspondent,
Patrick Hamkins

HAMKINS-- THAT VILE, NOSY HACK!
QUICK, OUTSIDE...!

Oh, LILY...
NOW THE WHOLE WORLD KNOWS WHO YOU ARE.

OH, MY WORD... IS THAT...?
YES, MR. SLUDGEWELL. THAT IS MY DAUGHTER.

If only I hadn't taken this from you...

SO... SO COLD!
OH NO! HAVE TO CLIMB EVEN HIGHER...
C-CAN'T SEE A THING...!
VISIBILITY... NIL.
NOOOO!
WHEW

THIS PASSAGE
IS GETTING THINNER
AND THINNER...

NO ROOM TO
TURN... CAN'T GO
HIGHER...

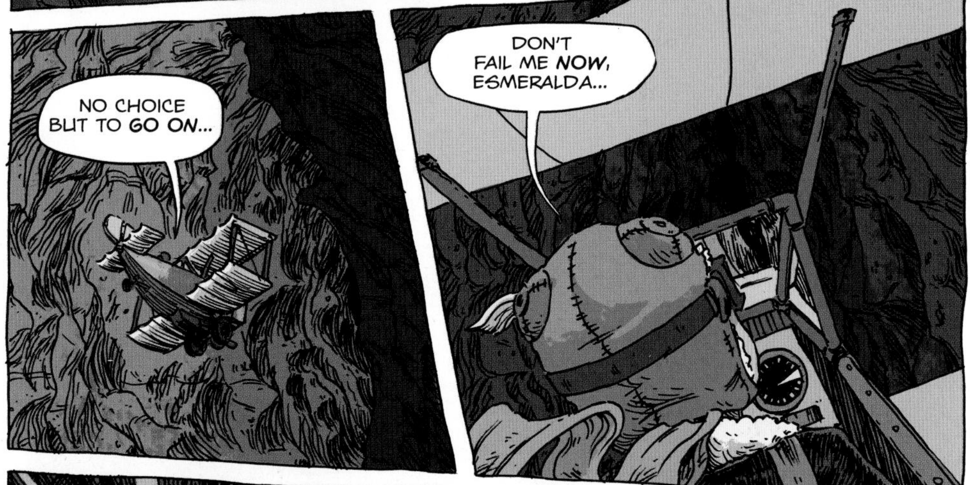
NO CHOICE
BUT TO GO ON...
DON'T
FAIL ME NOW,
ESMERALDA...

WRRRRROOOAM

WRAOWW

COME ON, GIRL. GET A GRIP ON YOURSELF.
IF OUR ORIENTATION IS CORRECT...

WHAT I'M LOOKING FOR IS *THIS WAY*...

HOW *VAST* IS THIS PLACE? IT MUST BE *TEN TIMES* THE SIZE OF THE PLAINS...

HOW DOES ANYTHING *EXIST* HERE? THERE'S NO FARMLAND, BARELY ANY TREES... HOW DOES ANYTHING *GROW?*

WHAT IF I *DON'T* FIND WHAT I'M LOOKING FOR? I'M GOING TO HAVE TO *PUT DOWN* SOON...

BUT HOW CAN I LAND *HERE?*

MAYBE I WAS *WRONG.* PERHAPS I *DIDN'T* SEE WHAT I *THOUGHT* I SAW...

MAYBE I'M *STUPID* AND *STUBBORN* AND I'LL *DIE* HERE...

...FAR FROM HOME...

...far from hogfolk who *love* me...

WAIT...

AM I **SEEING** THINGS?

MIGHT **JUST** HAVE ENOUGH FUEL...

ALLFATHER SKYPIG,
thankyouthankyou
thankyou

C'MON, C'MON...KEEP THAT NOSE UP!

AOWWW!
CRUNCH

TWANG

RRRRURRRURRURRRRRRRR

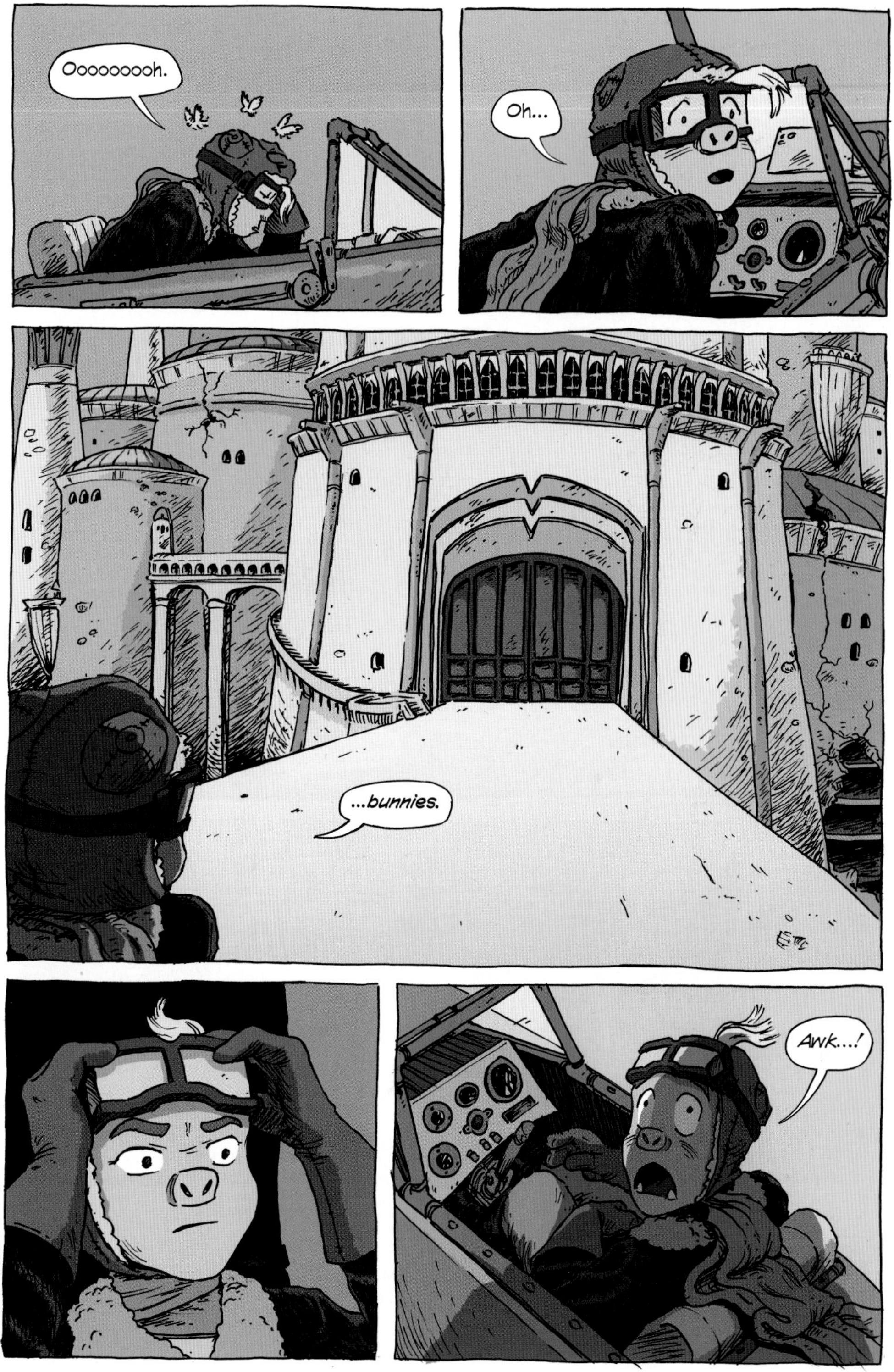

...bunnies.

OUT, PIGLET.
NOW.

I-- I COME IN PEACE. I ONLY WANT TO TALK.
SHUT UP.
MOVE.

WHERE ARE YOU TAKING ME?
I SAID SHUT UP, PIGLET.

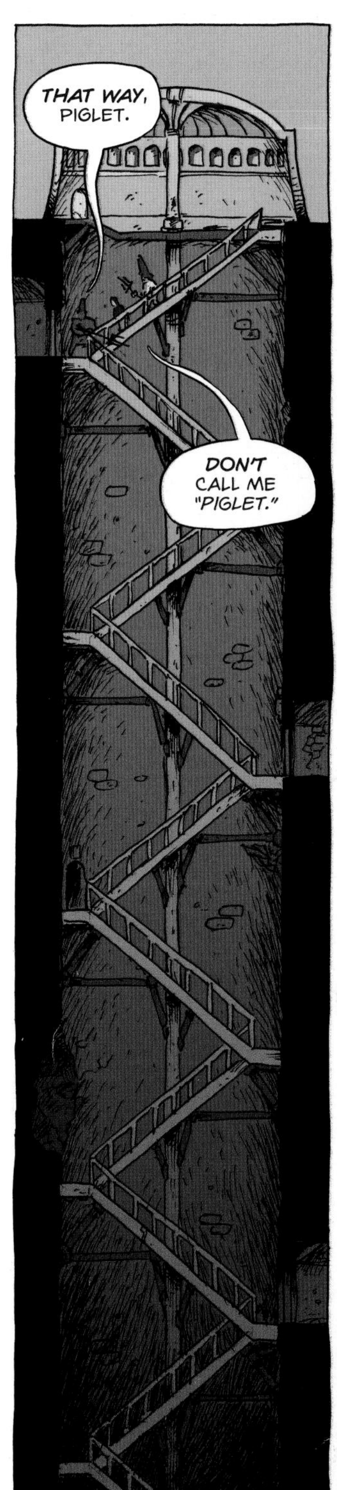
THAT WAY, PIGLET.
DON'T CALL ME "PIGLET."

HA HA HA HA HA HA HA

MOVE!

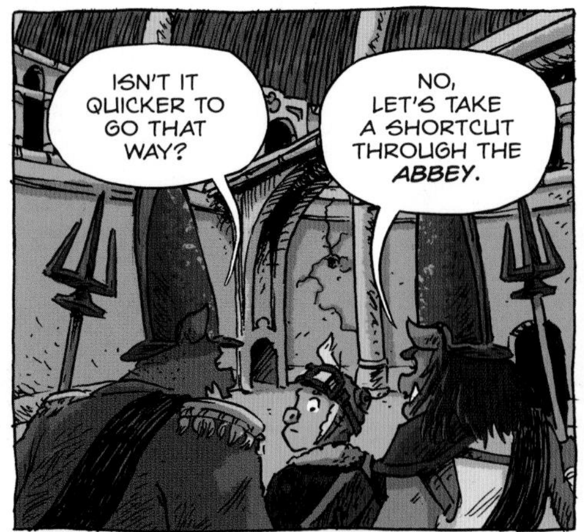
ISN'T IT QUICKER TO GO THAT WAY?
NO, LET'S TAKE A SHORTCUT THROUGH THE ABBEY.

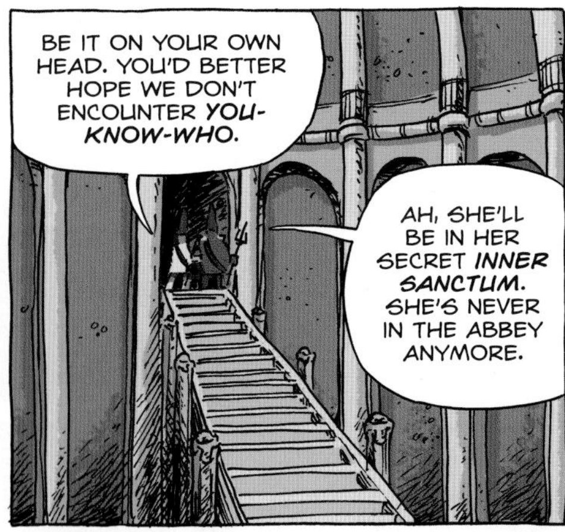
BE IT ON YOUR OWN HEAD. YOU'D BETTER HOPE WE DON'T ENCOUNTER YOU-KNOW-WHO.
AH, SHE'LL BE IN HER SECRET INNER SANCTUM. SHE'S NEVER IN THE ABBEY ANYMORE.

NOT SINCE EVERYONE LOST INTEREST...

SINCE THE CHIEF TOOK OVER.

SHE'S ONLY GOOD FOR BINDING SPELLS FOR HIM NOW...

THIS WAY...
MOVE!

DOESN'T THIS MEAN WE COME OUT IN *GARAGETOWN?*
YEAH, BUT THEN WE CAN TAKE THE *RAPID-RISER* TO HEADQUARTERS.
TRUE. GOOD IDEA.

THIS'LL BE AN *ADVENTURE* FOR OUR *LITTLE PIGGY* HERE, EH?
I'VE *TOLD* YOU-- YOU CALL ME *PIGGY* OR *PIGLET* ONE MORE TIME--

WHOA
WOOOOOOOOSH
HAHA HAHA!

HAHA!
YOU WERE *SAYING...?*

WELL, *WELL...*

I WAS EXPECTING *HERCULES FATCHOPS* OR MAYBE ONE OF HIS *CRONIES*, BUT *NOT* HIS *DAUGHTER*.
HELLO, LILY.
Oh, *bouncing bunnies*...
HAM!
HAM TROTTERS!

I REMEMBER YOU USED TO TALK TO ME ABOUT THE IDEA OF FLYING. YOU WERE SO PASSIONATE ABOUT IT.
AH, YES. I RECALL YOU WERE ALWAYS INTERESTED IN FLIGHT. SUCH AN INTELLIGENT AND FEISTY CHILD!

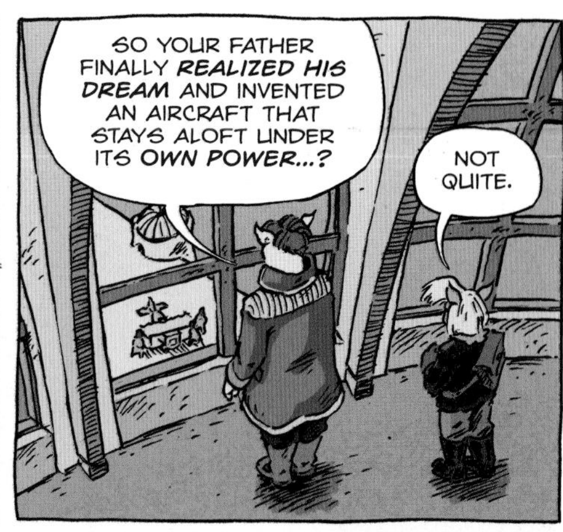
SO YOUR FATHER FINALLY REALIZED HIS DREAM AND INVENTED AN AIRCRAFT THAT STAYS ALOFT UNDER ITS OWN POWER...?
NOT QUITE.

IT WAS... UH, A TEAM EFFORT.
WHAT ARE THEY DOING WITH MY AIRCRAFT?
THEY'RE TAKING IT IN FOR SAFE-KEEPING.

THERE'S A STORM COMING IN, AND BELIEVE ME, YOU DON'T WANT TO LEAVE ANYTHING OUTSIDE IN THE KIND OF WEATHER THEY HAVE HERE.
IT'S AN ADVANCED DESIGN...

WHEN I LEFT THE PIGDOM, NOHOG HAD A CLUE... CERTAINLY NOT YOUR FATHER...
IT'S ALL IN THE LIFT-TO-DRAG RATIO. IT'S RUDDER AND WING DESIGN. IT'S ABOUT LIFT, NOT POWER...

RUDDER CONTROL. I RECALL HERCULES TALKING ABOUT THAT, AND HIS OTHER FAVORITE IDEA THAT "A PROPELLER IS A TRI-WINGED HUB ROTATING IN THE PERPENDICULAR."
WELL... IT IS.

INDEED.
SO... NO MAGICAL ENHANCEMENTS TO KEEP IT IN THE AIR?

NO. IT FLIES COMPLETELY UNDER ITS OWN POWER.
NONE AT ALL? INCREDIBLE.
AND HE MADE YOU THE PILOT.

ZORCH
AH, YES...

THAT WAS OBELIA.
I BELIEVE YOU'VE MET.

THAT WAS YOU? AT SWILLINGTON, ON THE GROUND?
AH, YES... I CAN'T MAKE UP MY MIND WHETHER YOU'RE A VERY BRAVE OR VERY STUPID LITTLE PIG, TAKING ON THREE OF OUR VESSELS.

PHINEAS WAS THERE, TOO. HE WAS PILOTING THE CRAFT THAT YOU BROUGHT DOWN...
...WITH GLUE BOMBS.

THANKS FOR THAT. HAD A VERY LONG WALK HOME.
I
OWE
YOU.

THAT'S A LITTLE JOKE. WE ACTUALLY PICKED HIM AND HIS CREW UP IN THE MOUNTAINS.
THEY WERE A BIT COLD, BUT WE'RE LUCKY IT'S SPRING. ANYWAY, THEY'RE A HARDY LOT, MY WARTHOGS. HANDPICKED, Y'KNOW.
'SRIGHT, CHIEF.

IT WAS QUITE A RESCUE OPERATION, THOUGH. COST US A LOT OF TIME AND EFFORT.
AND ALL BECAUSE OF ONE LITTLE PIG.

HOW DO YOU KNOW THERE'S JUST ONE OF ME?

FIRING UPON MY AIR VESSELS WAS AN ACT OF WAR.
WHY DID YOU COME HERE, LILY?

WHAT?
I'M TRYING TO STOP A WAR!

YOU CAME TO THE PIGDOM AND RAIDED US. YOU STOLE A GIANT WAREHOUSE FULL OF SUPPLIES. YOU STOLE A WHOLE MARKETPLACE!
HMM, NO. I LIKE TO SEE IT AS REDISTRIBUTION OF RESOURCES. TAKING FROM THE RICH TO GIVE TO THE POOR.

HEY, THAT'S ONE WAY OF JUSTIFYING IT. BUT THERE WERE CHILDREN IN THAT MARKETPLACE...
IT WAS A WONDER YOUR AIRCRAFT DIDN'T KILL ANYHOG.
"MARKETPLACE." THAT REMINDS ME...FOOD.
WHERE ARE MY MANNERS?

GRISELDA!

YOU MUST BE TIRED AND HUNGRY AFTER YOUR LONG FLIGHT.
WILL YOU JOIN ME FOR DINNER? I WANT TO HEAR ALL ABOUT YOUR ADVENTURES!
MASTER?

GRISELDA WILL SHOW YOU TO YOUR GUEST CHAMBERS AND ATTEND TO YOUR NEEDS. I'LL SEE YOU IN THE GRAND GALLERY IN AN HOUR.
YESSIR. THIS WAY-- MISS LILY, WAS IT?

GONNA BE A VICIOUS ONE...
YEAH. IF IT'S ANYTHING LIKE THE LAST STORM, WE WON'T BE ABLE TO FLY ANOTHER CAMPAIGN FOR A FEW DAYS...

BAROOOM

HERE WE ARE, MISS.
THERE'S A CHANGE OF CLOTHES IF YOU WANT THEM. THE WASHROOM'S THROUGH THAT FAR DOOR. IF YOU NEED ANYTHING ELSE, PLEASE RING THE BELL.
I'LL BE BACK TO FETCH YOU FOR SUPPER.

GRISELDA... AM I A PRISONER?

WE'RE ALL PRISONERS HERE, MISS.
BETTER HURRY UP. THE MASTER DOESN'T LIKE TO BE KEPT WAITING.

AH, NOW HERE'S A *TREAT*, LILY...
PERFECT *RODENTBACK LOAF*, ALL THE WAY FROM PIGGLESWICK.

I THOUGHT YOU'D ENJOY A *TASTE OF HOME*.
ALL THIS FOOD IS FROM THE *RAID* AT PIGGLESWICK?

NOT *ALL* OF IT. BUT THE LOCAL PRODUCE IS *POOR PICKINGS*-- SIMPLE FARE, MOSTLY, WHEN THEY CAN GET IT TO *GROW*.
YOU WOULDN'T BELIEVE IT FROM *THIS* WEATHER, BUT THERE HAVE BEEN DROUGHTS, PESTILENCE. CROPS FAILED, LIVESTOCK DIED.

THERE WOULD'VE BEEN A FULL-ON *FAMINE* IF *I* HADN'T ARRIVED.
I *SAVED* THESE WARTHOGFOLK BY *BUILDING AIRCRAFT* SO THAT WE COULD GO AND *FIND FOOD*.

SKY CHARIOTS, THEY CALLED THEM-- AND YET I COULDN'T HAVE BUILT THEM WITHOUT THEIR *HELP*.
WITH THEIR *KNOWLEDGE*, I SOLVED SO MANY OF THE *PROBLEMS* I'D HAD WITH MY AIRCRAFT DESIGNS.

BUT YOU USE *MAGIC* TO KEEP THEM IN THE AIR-- IN THE *ENGINE DESIGN*, IN THE *CONSTRUCTION*, *EVERYTHING*.

AH, YES I DO, LILY. BUT DON'T LABOR UNDER THE MISAPPREHENSION THAT MY PRIMARY OBJECTIVE WAS TO CREATE FLYING MACHINES USING PURE SCIENCE.
I CONTEND THAT THE TWO EXIST SIDE BY SIDE FOR A REASON, PERHAPS ONE THE ALLFATHER INTENDED US TO DISCOVER.

HERE, THE MAGIC IS EVERYWHERE-- IT'S IN THE ROCKS, IN THE AIR, IT'S ALL AROUND US.
IT'S SO MUCH STRONGER HERE. SUCH AN ABUNDANT RESOURCE. YOU CAN HARNESS IT AND USE IT.

WHEN I FIRST CAME HERE, THE WARTHOGS WERE STARVING. I LED THEM, AND THEY FOLLOWED.
WITH OUR SKY CHARIOTS, MY AIR VESSELS, WE BEGAN JOURNEYING FARTHER AND FARTHER...

AND NOW YOU'RE COMING TO THE PIGDOM?
LILY, IT'S OURS FOR THE TAKING.
WE NEED TO SHOW THEM WHAT WE KNOW. WHAT I KNOW.

HAM, LISTEN TO ME.
HOGFOLK LIVE THERE, PEACEFULLY, WITH EACH OTHER, WITH ALL THE ISLANDS IN THE ARCHIPELAGO. YOU CAN'T JUST MARCH IN AND TAKE WHAT THEY HAVE.

WHY NOT? PIGS ARE SMALLER AND WEAKER THAN WARTHOGS.
WE'LL INVADE, YOU'LL SERVE US, AND WE'LL ALL BUILD A WHOLE NEW WORLD USING MAGIC AND SCIENCE...

...WE CAN MAKE IT BETTER FOR EVERYHOG!
FOR ALL PIGKIND!

WHAT, WITH YOU IN CHARGE?
BETTER THAN THE LIKES OF YOUR FATHER AND THAT FAT, POMPOUS FOOL, PIGMINISTER FLANKSFORD!

HAM, I HAVE MY PROBLEMS WITH MY FATHER, TOO...
BUT IT DOESN'T NEED TO BE LIKE THIS. IF YOU JUST TALKED TO THE PIGDOM, THEY COULD HELP THE WARTHOGS...
WHAT, LIKE YOUR FATHER TALKED TO ME... RIDICULED ME, MY IDEAS? HAD ME HOUNDED FROM THE PIGDOM?

HE DIDN'T HOUND YOU. HE HAD RULES...YOU BROKE THEM.
IT WAS YOU WHO WENT TO THE NEWSPAPERS. HE ANSWERED YOUR ACCUSATIONS, BUT IF ANYONE HOUNDED YOU, IT WAS THE PRESS...

LOOK, HE CAN BE A BOOR, I KNOW THAT BETTER THAN ANYONE. BUT HIS HEART'S IN THE RIGHT PLACE...

HAM, YOU INSPIRED ME. YOU WERE MY FATHER'S BRIGHTEST STUDENT...

DON'T CALL ME THAT.
I'M NOT ANYHOG'S STUDENT, LEAST OF ALL YOUR FATHER'S.

SORRY. JUST WANTED TO SAY THAT YOU'RE AN INSPIRATION... TO ME, AND, UH, MY ENGINEERS.

DON'T TRY TO SWEET-TALK ME, GIRL...
I'M NOT. IT'S TRUE.

YOU KNOW WHY I CAME HERE, LILY? I CAME BECAUSE IT CALLED ME. I COULD FEEL IT.
I FLEW HERE.
I BUILT A NEW MACHINE WITH ALL THE MAGICAL ENHANCEMENTS I COULD MUSTER AND IT TOOK ME FARTHER THAN ANY PIG HAS EVER BEEN!
ALL THE WHILE, I WAS CONVINCED... I KNEW... THAT NO MACHINE COULD EVER FLY WITHOUT THE HELP OF MAGIC. I KNEW THAT IN THE VERY PIT OF MY SOUL.

THEN YOU FLY IN HERE WITH THAT MACHINE OF YOUR FATHER'S... PROVING THAT IT IS POSSIBLE.
BY THE ALLFATHER, YOU ARE YOUR FATHER'S DAUGHTER, ALL RIGHT.

I DON'T AGREE WITH HIM ON EVERY DETAIL. I'M SURE THERE'S A WAY OF MIXING BOTH DISCIPLINES TO GET A BETTER RESULT.
ONE OF MY, ER-- ASSISTANTS WOULD AGREE WITH YOU. BUT I THINK HE MIGHT HAVE AN ISSUE WITH THE TYPE OF MAGIC YOU USE.

YOU'RE YOUNG, LILY. YOU'RE HIGHLY INTELLIGENT, QUITE OBVIOUSLY FEARLESS...
...AND BEAUTIFUL, TOO.

I WONDER WHAT IT WOULD BE LIKE IF YOU AND I COULD TALK PROPERLY, AWAY FROM ALL THESE OTHER CONCERNS...
BUT THERE'S A LOT YOU DON'T KNOW ABOUT THE WORLD.

I'M TIRED. THERE'S LOTS TO DO IN THE MORNING. WE'LL RECONVENE THEN.
GRISELDA, WOULD YOU SEE MISS LEANCHOPS BACK TO HER CHAMBERS?
YES, MASTER.

THIS WAY, PLEASE, LADY LILY.

LILY... SPIES GET EXECUTED IN TIMES OF WAR, YOU KNOW.

I'M NOT A SPY, HAM.
THINK OF ME AS A PEACE ENVOY. I'M AN INDEPENDENT OPERATOR.

IF YOU REMEMBER ANYTHING ABOUT ME, YOU SHOULD KNOW THAT.

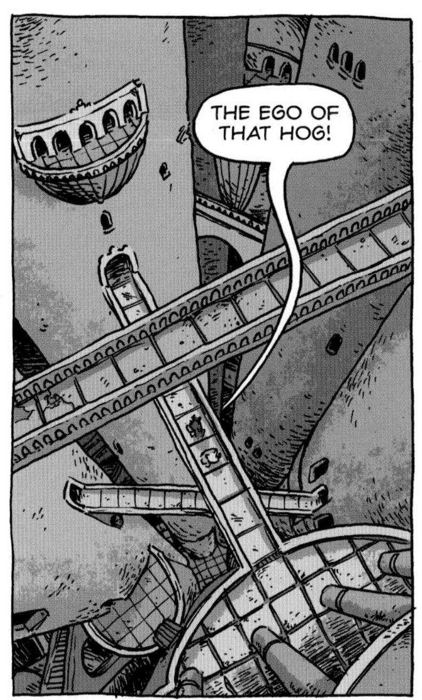
THE EGO OF THAT HOG!

THIS PLACE IS *INCREDIBLE!*

WAIT, GRISELDA... THIS ISN'T THE WAY WE CAME...
NO, MILADY. WE'RE TAKING THE **SCENIC** ROUTE.

WHY?
HEY, IF IT ISN'T A LITTLE *PIGGY-WIGGY!*

A *PIGGY* AND A *DWARFHOG!*
I HEARD A *RUMOR A LITTLE PINK PIGLET* FLEW IN.
AS IF PIGS KNEW HOW TO *FLY!*
PLEASE LET US PASS.

WHAT IF WE *DON'T*, DWARFHOG?
WHERE ARE YOU GOING IN SUCH A HURRY?
STAY. *ENTERTAIN* US!
WON'T ASK AGAIN.

NO. PLAY WITH US!
STAY *BEHIND ME*, MILADY.

CHUNK
OOOOONG
KSSSH

AAAAAA
OOWWW
CRAK

KRAK
UFFFF

KRAK
GNNN

PWAAF

oooh

LADY LILY--
RUN!

COME ON, YOU MORONS!
AFTER THEM!

POK
POK

YOU WERE LUCKY THE FIRST TIME, SHORTY...

...EH?
VANISHED. BLOODY WITCHES!

A SECRET PASSAGEWAY!
THIS ANCIENT CITADEL IS HONEYCOMBED WITH THEM, MILADY, BUT FEW KNOW THEY EVEN EXIST.

I'M SORRY YOU HAD TO EXPERIENCE THAT, MILADY.
SOCIETY HERE IS CRUMBLING. GANGS LIKE THAT ARE BECOMING MORE COMMON-PLACE.
SUDDENLY, YOU'RE VERY TALKATIVE.

I'M SORRY. IT WAS DANGEROUS FOR ME TO SPEAK OUT IN THE OPEN.

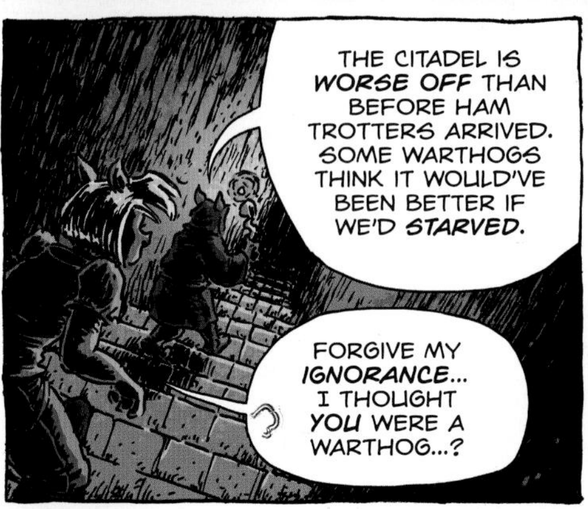
THE CITADEL IS WORSE OFF THAN BEFORE HAM TROTTERS ARRIVED. SOME WARTHOGS THINK IT WOULD'VE BEEN BETTER IF WE'D STARVED.
FORGIVE MY IGNORANCE... I THOUGHT YOU WERE A WARTHOG...?

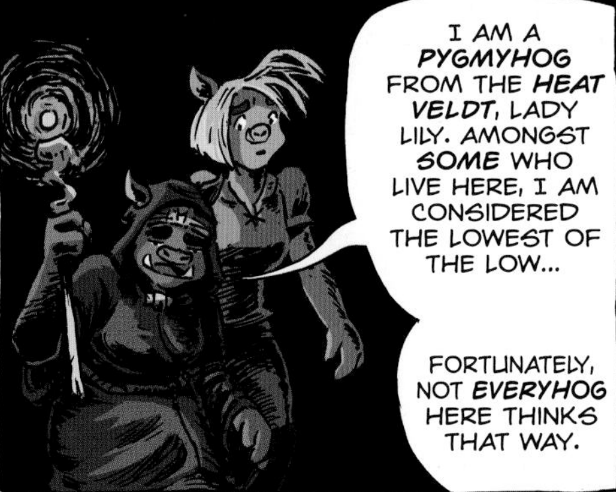
I AM A PYGMYHOG FROM THE HEAT VELDT, LADY LILY. AMONGST SOME WHO LIVE HERE, I AM CONSIDERED THE LOWEST OF THE LOW...
FORTUNATELY, NOT EVERYHOG HERE THINKS THAT WAY.

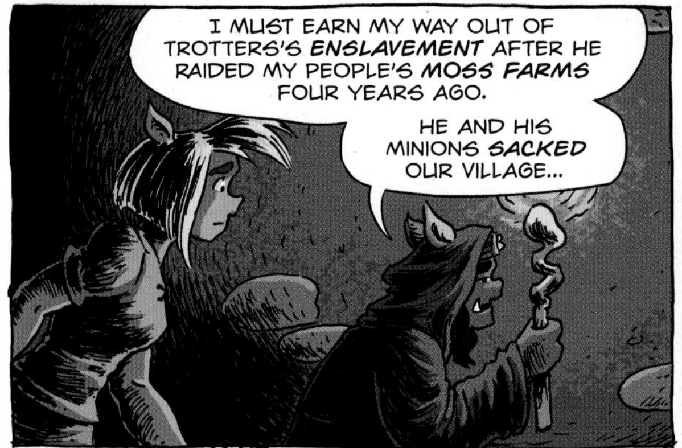
I MUST EARN MY WAY OUT OF TROTTERS'S ENSLAVEMENT AFTER HE RAIDED MY PEOPLE'S MOSS FARMS FOUR YEARS AGO.
HE AND HIS MINIONS SACKED OUR VILLAGE...

HE TOOK ALMOST EVERYTHING THEY HAD...
EVEN THEIR CHIEFTAIN...

...ME.
I GAVE MYSELF SO THAT HE WOULD SPARE MY TRIBE.

I STILL DO NOT KNOW IF THEY SURVIVED. THEY NEEDED SUPPLIES TO LAST THE DRY SEASON...
SOMEDAY, I HOPE TO GO BACK...

THAT'S... THAT'S HORRIBLE.
THIS IS ALL TOO MUCH TO TAKE IN.
THIS WAY. NOT FAR, NOW.

THE MOST HIGH WISHES TO MEET YOU...

DO NOT FEAR. WE MEAN NO HARM.
SHE WILL EXPLAIN EVERYTHING.

SHE, LIKE ME, HAS BEEN DISPLACED AS LEADER OF HER PEOPLE... OF THIS CITADEL.
OF THE TWO OF US, SHE HAS IT WORSE. SHE HAS TO WATCH HER PEOPLE SUFFER. AT LEAST I AM SPARED THAT.

AFTER YOU, LADY LILY.

I AM SISTER CIRCE, MAGICSTRIX AND HIGH BIBLIOTAPH OF THE TEMPLE OF THE SKYPIGS.
WELCOME TO OUR SANCTUM.
Er... Hello. I'm Lily Leanchops.

I KNOW WHO YOU ARE, LADY LILY. THE CIRCLE FORETOLD OF YOUR COMING. FRET NOT-- YOU ARE SAFE HERE.
THE CIRCLE...?
THE EYE OF THE SKYPIGS.

SKYPIGS? MORE THAN ONE? MORE THAN THE ALLFATHER?
YES. DO YOU KNOW THE LEGEND OF THE FIRST OF US-- THE EARLIEST HOGS?

THERE WAS NO PIGKIND, NO WARTHOG, NO WILDBOAR, NO HIGHLAND SWINETRIBES, NO KILLERCOB HORDES OR SOWMAZONS...
WE WERE ALL AS ONE.

I KNOW THAT THE ALLFATHER SKYPIG IS SUPPOSED TO HAVE COME TO EARTH AND DELIVERED OUR ANCESTORS HERE.
THE ALLFATHER FELL FROM THE HEAVENS AFTER A GREAT BATTLE WITH THE SKY GODS, WHO TRIED TO WREST HIS PRECIOUS CARGO FROM HIM.

HE WAS INJURED BUT HE MADE THE GROUND FERTILE SO THAT THE CARGO-- HIS CHILDREN-- COULD LIVE IN PEACE AND ABUNDANCE.
THAT IS ONE TELLING OF THE MYTH, YES.
BUT DID YOU KNOW THAT THE ALLFATHER HAD A WIFE?

THIS IS SHE--
THE DISTANT, ANCESTRAL MOTHER OF US ALL.

EVEN OF OBELIA AND PHINEAS. EVEN THE ARMY OF FOOLS WHO ANSWER TO THEM.
EVEN SUCH AS THEY. EVEN HAM TROTTERS.

THE ALLMOTHER VANISHES FROM MANY OF THE ANCIENT TEXTS THAT WERE CARRIED FORTH TO DISTANT LANDS-- BUT WE MAINTAIN THE OLDER STORIES HERE, IN THE TEMPLE.

SO IT IS SAID, THE ALLMOTHER BIT OFF HER OWN WINGS AND PARTED FROM HER LOVE, THE ALLFATHER, TO STAY ON SOLID GROUND AND TEND TO HER CHILDREN, WHILE HE RETURNED TO THE SKY.
IS THAT TRUE?

LADY LILY, IT IS MYTH. EVEN OUR RECORDS HERE IN THE CITADEL DO NOT GO BACK TO THE BEGINNING OF HISTORY.
IT WAS RETOLD MANY TIMES, FROM GENERATION TO GENERATION, BEFORE IT WAS EVER WRITTEN DOWN.

TRUTH IS REVEALED THROUGH INTERPRETATION OF MYTH, WHICH IS AS IT SHOULD BE.
EVEN IF THERE IS AN ALLFATHER SKYPIG ABOVE... AND I BELIEVE THERE IS... AND EVEN IF MY GREATEST, GREAT-GRANDMOTHER WAS THE ALLMOTHER SKYPIG, WE MUST STILL BE RESPONSIBLE FOR OUR OWN ACTIONS.

THIS IS WHERE I HAVE ERRED WITH HAM TROTTERS. I SHOWED HIM POWER...
MAGIC HAS CRAZED AND CONSUMED HIM AND NOW HE IS OBSESSED WITH WHAT IT BRINGS TO HIS INVENTIONS.
THAT'S NOT YOUR FAULT.

HE ALWAYS WANTED FAST RESULTS. WHEN HE WORKED FOR MY FATHER, DAD INSISTED THEY FOLLOW SCIENTIFIC METHODS.
SCIENCE, I FANCY, NEEDS A CERTAIN FAITH IN THE PROCESS OF OBSERVATION AND EXPERIMENTATION THAT REVEALS FACT.

UM... THE DIFFERENCE BETWEEN MAGICAL AND SCIENTIFIC APPROACHES SEEM FAIRLY SIMPLE TO ME. SCIENCE IS EVERYTHING YOU'VE TESTED AND DISCOVERED... AND EVERYTHING YOU BUILD FROM WHAT YOU'VE LEARNED LASTS.
ANYTHING YOU BUILD WITH MAGIC IS SHORT-LIVED.

INDEED. SCIENCE AND MAGIC ARE MORE ALIKE THAN MANY ACKNOWLEDGE.
BUT THE SHORT-LIVED QUALITY OF MAGIC SUGGESTS...?
THAT IT IS A TOOL.

MAGIC IS IMPERMANENCE. EVERYTHING IS IMPERMANENT, BUT MAGIC IS THE PRESENT, THE NOW. SCIENCE BUILDS BRIDGES INTO THE FUTURE. AND IT IS THE FUTURE THAT WE MUST PROTECT.

TROTTERS FOUND US WHEN WE WERE WEAK.
OUR ONCE-PROUD CIVILIZATION HAD SUFFERED DISASTER AFTER DISASTER.

THE LAND WAS BLIGHTED. SUDDENLY WE COULDN'T SUSTAIN OURSELVES.

THE DAYS WERE DARK. WE WERE AILING.
ONE DAY, HAM TROTTERS ARRIVED IN HIS SKY CHARIOT.

IT CRASHED, HE WAS INJURED. WE TOOK HIM IN AND NURSED HIM BACK TO HEALTH...

TROTTERS TALKED, AND PROMISED TO HELP. HE PROMISED BETTER THINGS TO ALL WARTHOGS.

WE WERE DESPERATE... BUT I WAS FOOLISH.
I INVITED HIM IN. I TRUSTED HIM.

I SAW THAT HE HAD HIS OWN BASIC APTITUDE WITH MAGIC, AND I GUIDED HIM, TAUGHT HIM TO HONE HIS ABILITIES.

HE DID, ALL THE WHILE SEEDING RUMOR AND MISTRUST AGAINST THE LEADERSHIP OF THIS CITADEL. AND WHEN HE SAW HIS MOMENT, HE SEIZED CONTROL.

MY HOGFOLK TURNED AWAY FROM THE OLD WAYS...
THEY NEEDED HOPE...AND TROTTERS GAVE THEM HOPE.

FALSE HOPE, BY THE SOUNDS OF IT.
AND NOW HE PLANS TO TAKE OVER THE PIGDOM...
HE ALREADY TOLD YOU THIS? SUCH CONFIDENCE.

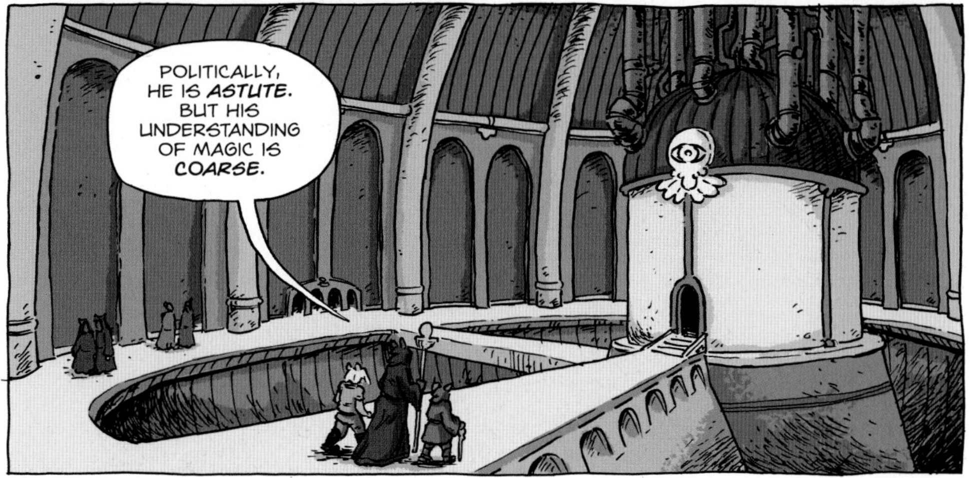
POLITICALLY, HE IS ASTUTE. BUT HIS UNDERSTANDING OF MAGIC IS COARSE.

HE WILL ENSLAVE YOUR PEOPLE, LADY LILY.
WE BELIEVE THIS WAS ALWAYS HIS PLAN. TO GROW STRONGER HERE, THEN RETURN TO HIS OWN LAND TO CLAIM YOUR LEADER'S HEADS.

MY FATHER SAID HAM WAS ONLY EVER IMAGINATIVE WHEN IT CAME TO HIS OWN AMBITION.
YOUR FATHER IS INSIGHTFUL.
Sigh
SOMETIMES HE HAS A LISTENING PROBLEM, TOO...

TROTTERS HAS RAISED AN ARMY AGAINST THE PIGDOM. TOGETHER WITH HIS SKY CHARIOTS...
IT'LL BE SLAUGHTER-- ON BOTH SIDES.

I WONDER IF I'LL EVER SEE MY FAMILY AGAIN.
THAT IS PART OF THE REASON WHY WE HAVE COME HERE, LADY LILY.
COME... LET ME SHOW YOU THE CIRCLE...

WELCOME TO THE EYE OF THE SKYPIGS.
THIS IS THE INNERMOST HEART OF THE TEMPLE, AND THE CITADEL ITSELF.

EACH ARE A PART OF THE WHOLE.

TROTTERS HAS A RAW TALENT FOR TAPPING NON-CARDINAL MAGIC, BUT HE USES IT MERELY AS A POWER SOURCE, AS ENERGY.

HE DOES NOT RESPECT IT. HE DOES NOT COMPREHEND THAT IT IS ALIVE AND THAT IT MAY BURN HIM...

...OR MEMBERS OF MY TRIBE, CITIZENS OF THIS CITADEL, AND MANY OTHERS BEYOND THESE LANDS.

I HAVE FAILED TO PROTECT THEM ALL.

WE CANNOT CHANGE THE PAST, AND THE FUTURE IS UNWRITTEN, SO THE ONLY ASPECT OF LIVING WE HAVE INFLUENCE OVER IS THE PRESENT.

THERE IS ALWAYS THE CONSTANCY OF CHANGE, THE CERTAINTY OF CHANCE AND RENEWAL. BUT WE MUSTN'T ABANDON WISDOM FOR WAR.
WHAT SHOULD I LOOK FOR, LADY LILY? WHO?

IS THIS HOW YOU KNEW I WAS COMING HERE? CAN IT TELL THE FUTURE?
NO. IT IS NOT AN ORACLE OF PREDICTION, EXACTLY... MORE OF DEEPENED PERCEPTIONS.

IT WILL SHOW US YOUR LOVED ONES, PERHAPS...
DAD! HE LOOKS SO TIRED.
DAD, WHY WOULDN'T YOU LET ME HELP YOU?

AUNTIE SASHA! SHE'S A MOTHER TO ME... SHE'S SO LOVELY. SHE KNOWS MAGIC, YOU KNOW!
I CAN FEEL THAT SHE'S AN ADEPT...

IS THERE A WAY WE CAN HEAR WHAT THEY'RE SAYING?
STRANGE. WE SHOULD ALREADY BE ABLE TO. YOUR EMOTIONAL CONNECTION TO THEM IS STRONG. AND YET...

WHAT'S HAPPENING...?
THERE IS... INTERFERENCE...

ARCHIE!
NO. SOMETHING ELSE...

I MUST CONTAIN--
CIIIIRCCEEEE...
SHROOOM

SHROOOOOM

MMMPH
UHHHH
OOONG

THE DARK! THE DARKNESS!
AAAAAAA...
SHROOOOOM
MMMPH!

MMMPAAH!
SHLOPP

WH-WHAT WAS THAT?
DEATH, DARKNESS. SOMETHING VERY POWERFUL. SOMETHING NOT OF THE NOW.
BUT MAGICSTRIX, SUCH A FORCE COULD NOT ACCESS THE EYE OF THE SKYPIGS. IT'S IMPOSSIBLE!

"NOT OF THE NOW"? YOU SAID THIS THING DIDN'T SEE INTO THE FUTURE?
IT DOESN'T. THAT WAS AN INCURSION FROM OUTSIDE TIME...
MAGICSTRIX! TROTTERS IS FORCING HIS WAY INTO THE TEMPLE!

TROTTERS HAS SPIES... ONE OF THEM MUST'VE REPORTED THAT LILY DID NOT RETURN TO HER GUEST CHAMBERS.
GO. I WILL DELAY HIM.

HE WILL NOT ARGUE WITH ME. HE STILL NEEDS ME TO BIND HIS SUPER-SPELLS FOR HIM.

COME, LADY LILY. THIS WAY IS SAFE.

MAGICSTRIX, THEY WOULDN'T **LISTEN.** THEY **SMASHED THE DOOR IN!**
PLEASE DO NOT ENTER THIS **HOLY PLACE** WITH **ANGER** IN YOUR HEARTS.
BACK, YOU **WORTHLESS BOOKWORMS!**

CIRCE. WHERE IS LILY LEANCHOPS?
THE YOUNG PIG WITH **WINGS OF HER OWN MAKING?** HOW **CARELESS** OF YOU TO LOSE HER.

DON'T PLAY GAMES WITH ME, CIRCE. THIS IS THE ONLY PLACE SHE COULD BE.
IN ALL OF THE CITADEL? I THINK **NOT.**

SHLAP

HAM, YOUR SHOW OF STRENGTH IS UNNECESSARY AND **UNWISE...**
WHERE IS SHE?

CHIEF... Apparently she's back in her room.

CIRCE...TOMORROW, A NEW AGE FOR THE WARTHOGS OF THE CELESTIAL BLUE CITADEL WILL ARRIVE.
SOON, I WILL CONTROL THE WILDERNESS **AND** THE PIGDOM PLAINS. AND WE WILL EXTEND OUR REACH **FURTHER.**

I NEED YOU TO HELP CAST THE FINAL BINDING SPELL OF MY AIR FLOTILLA.
BUT I WILL NOT NEED YOUR SERVICES FOREVER. IT IS BY MY DISCRETION THAT YOU RETAIN RELATIVE FREEDOM...

REMEMBER THAT.
HAM, YOU WILL ALWAYS NEED ME. YOU WILL ALWAYS NEED TWO TO MAKE ANY LARGE SPELLBINDING CEREMONY WORK.

YOUR SKY CHARIOTS WILL NOT FLY WITHOUT MY HELP.
YOU'RE WRONG. I'M ALREADY AS POWERFUL AS YOU, CIRCE.

SHROMM
AND I'M GROWING STRONGER BY THE MOMENT.

Mmmh

LILY...

!
HOW LONG HAVE YOU BEEN HERE?

I... JUST NOW... I...
...WAS WALKING...

JUST...GOT SOME **CLARITY**. FOUND MYSELF **HERE**.
WANTED TO **TALK** TO YOU.

HAM...?
Nnngh
IT'S LIKE... THERE ARE **CLOUDS** IN MY **MIND**...

FROM WHAT I **REMEMBER**, WE DIDN'T RENEW OUR **ACQUAINTANCE** IN QUITE THE **RIGHT WAY** YESTERDAY.
Well, I... I...

YOU **UNDERSTAND** ME, LILY. YOU UNDERSTAND **THE DREAM**.

SO **BEAUTIFUL**...
THE PROPER NAME OF THIS PLACE IS **THE CITADEL OF THE CELESTIAL BLUE**.

THEY SAY IT WAS ONCE DECKED OUT IN JADE AND AZURE TILES TO PROPERLY REFLECT THE GLORY OF THE **SKY**-- OUR CRADLE.

THIS IS SUPPOSED TO BE THE **EXACT POINT** WHERE THE ALLFATHER AND ALLMOTHER **LANDED**.

THIS PLACE WAS BUILT IN **MEMORY** OF THEM. OF THE **FLYING PIGS** WHO ARE SUPPOSEDLY OUR **ANCESTORS**...

EVER SINCE I WAS A SMALL BOAR, I DREAMED OF **FLYING**. I **LONGED** FOR IT.
ME, TOO.

I WENT DOWN TO THE GARAGE, HAD A LOOK AT YOUR AIRCRAFT. IT'S A BEAUTIFUL MACHINE, LILY.

YOU BUILT IT, DIDN'T YOU...?
NOW YOU SEEM MORE LIKE THE HAM TROTTERS I REMEMBER...

WE WERE BOTH A LOT YOUNGER THEN, LILY.
HAM, PLEASE TELL ME WHAT'S WRONG. MAYBE I CAN HELP.

Clouds... like thunder-clouds...
I KNOW YOU GET IT, LILY. YOU ALWAYS DID.

YOU SEE, THAT'S IT, LILY... THAT'S ALL IT IS...
HAM, WHAT'S WRONG?

I JUST WANT TO FLY. THAT'S ALL I EVER WANTED...
...TO FLY.

HAM!
NNNGGH

BY THE END OF TODAY, EVERYTHING WILL HAVE CHANGED.

LOOK OUT THERE, LILY. WHAT DO YOU SEE?
I-I...

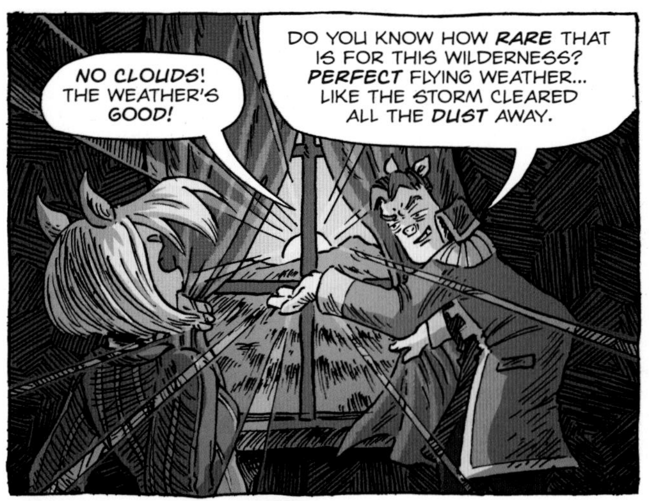
NO CLOUDS! THE WEATHER'S GOOD!
DO YOU KNOW HOW RARE THAT IS FOR THIS WILDERNESS? PERFECT FLYING WEATHER... LIKE THE STORM CLEARED ALL THE DUST AWAY.

IT'S A GOOD OMEN! YOU CAN SEE FOREVER!
YOU SEE, LILY, TODAY IS THE DAY.

TODAY IS THE DAY WE INVADE THE PIGDOM PLAINS!
HAM... NO!

JOIN ME, LILY. BE ON THE WINNING SIDE!
IMAGINE WHEN YOUR FATHER SEES US BOTH SOARING IN ON THE KIND OF AIRCRAFT HE CAN ONLY DREAM OF INVENTING!

JUST IMAGINE HIS HUMILIATION!
HAM, YOU'RE HURTING MY ARM.

AS WELL AS THE SKY CHARIOTS, THERE IS A GROUND FORCE OF WARTHOGS WAITING IN THE MOUNTAINS. ONCE THE AIR FLOTILLA HAS TAKEN OUT ALL RESISTANCE, I'LL SEND UP A FLARE.
HAM, PLEASE LET GO OF ME.

THAT'S THE SIGNAL FOR THEM TO SWARM DOWN AND INVADE. THE PIGDOM WILL NEVER KNOW WHAT'S HIT IT.
HAM...

LET GO.

OH NO...
BY THE WINGED ONE, THE CLOUDS... THEY'VE CLEARED!
LILY, LISTEN TO ME...

YOU HAVE TO GET OUT OF HERE. BEFORE IT COMES BACK.
HAM, WHAT IN SEVEN SHADES OF PIGSHINE IS GOING ON?
ONE MOMENT YOU'RE A RAVING LUNAHOG, THE NEXT YOU'RE BACK TO NORMAL...

NO TIME TO EXPLAIN. YOU NEED TO WARN THE PIGDOM ABOUT THE INVASION.
HERE, IF ANYHOG TRIES TO STOP YOU, FLASH THIS SIGNATURE AT THEM.

YOUR AIRCRAFT IS IN THE MAIN COURT GARAGE BENEATH US. TAKE THE MAIN RAPID-RISER ALONG THE CORRIDOR.
RUN, WARN THE PIGDOM...

HHKKKKKKK

GO, LILY. CAN ONLY RESIST IT FOR A SHORT TIME...

OH!
LOOK OUT, LADY LILY...!

WHERE D'YOU THINK YOU'RE GOING IN SUCH A *HURRY*, PIGGIKINS?
whew

TO GET *HELP*. YOUR *CHIEF* IS HAVING SOME KIND OF FIT.
A FIT?

SEE FOR YOURSELVES. YOU'D BETTER LOOK AFTER HIM, OR ELSE THERE'LL BE *HELL TO PAY!*
CHIEF!

CHIEF, WHAT'S *WRONG?*
ARE YOU ALL RIGHT?

I THINK, PERHAPS, AN *ESCAPE* IS BEING MADE...?
YEAH. AND I'M VERY *GRATEFUL* FOR YOUR HELP.

NOW *HIT ME OVER THE HEAD* AND I'LL SAY YOU *OVERPOWERED* ME.
I CAN'T DO *THAT!*

YOU *HAVE* TO! OTHERWISE MY COVER AS A LOYAL, VANQUISHED SERF WILL BE *BLOWN*.
COME *WITH ME.*

TO THE GARAGE?
NO, SILLY. TO THE *PIGDOM PLAINS!*

OPEN THIS DOOR!
BAM
BAM

I CAN FIT YOU INTO MY AIRCRAFT'S **CARGO LOCKER.** IT MIGHT BE A BIT **UNCOMFORTABLE**, BUT WE COULD DO IT...
I'VE GOT A **BETTER IDEA.**

THE MAGICSTRIX AND I WATCHED YOU FLY YOUR AIRCRAFT IN WITH ALL THE **SKILL** AND **GRACE** OF A BIRD.
YOU DON'T NEED **SKILL** TO PILOT ONE OF TROTTERS'S SKY CHARIOTS. YOU JUST POINT THE THING WHERE YOU WANT TO GO AND THE VESSEL TAKES YOU THERE.

I BET I COULD FOLLOW YOU HOME!
AND THEN I'D HAVE **PROOF** TO CONVINCE **DAD'S PEERS** THAT THE INVASION IS ON ITS WAY...!

WE'VE GOT NOTHING TO LOSE!

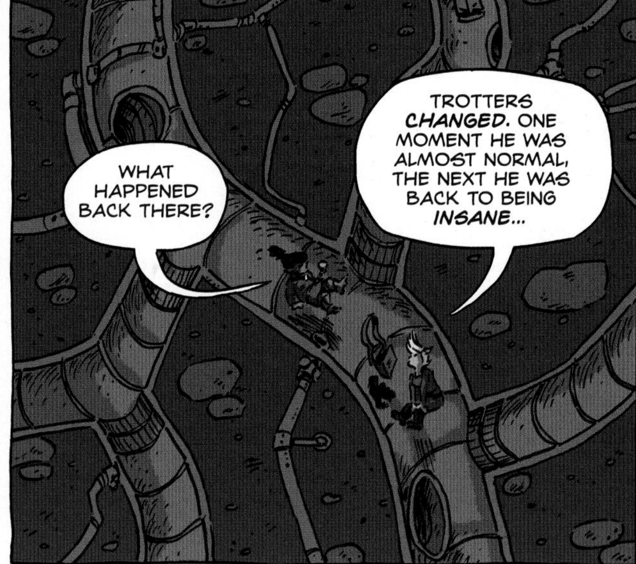
WHAT HAPPENED BACK THERE?
TROTTERS **CHANGED.** ONE MOMENT HE WAS ALMOST NORMAL, THE NEXT HE WAS BACK TO BEING **INSANE...**

TROTTERS IS CONSUMED BY NON-CARDINAL MAGIC. IT INFECTS EVERYTHING HE DOES.
I'VE HEARD STORIES LIKE THAT FROM MY AUNTIE SASHA...
BUT NO... THIS IS... DIFFERENT. SOMETHING MORE...

...SOMETHING WORSE.

NOHOG ABOUT. DON'T THINK THE ALARM'S BEEN RAISED YET.
LET'S GO THIS WAY... FEWER GUARDS.
MAYBE WE CAN MAKE IT TO THE GARAGE WITHOUT BEING SEEN.

WE'RE OUT OF LUCK. THOUGHT THIS BACK WAY INTO THE GARAGE WOULD BE UNGUARDED.
LEAVE THIS TO ME.

HEY, YOU!
THIS AREA'S OFF-LIMITS TO CIVILIANS.

THE CHIEF HIMSELF HAS GIVEN MY ESCORT AND I THE FREEDOM OF THE CITADEL.
YOUR ESCORT?

YES-- GRISELDA, THE GREAT CHIEF'S PERSONAL SERF.
COME ON, GRISELDA, I WANT TO SEE THE GARAGE!
IT'S THE CHIEF'S SEAL, ALL RIGHT.

YES, IT IS. WILL YOU LET US THROUGH, PLEASE?
UH...

I DON'T WANT TO HAVE TO REPORT BACK TO HIM THAT OUR WAY WAS OBSTRUCTED BY TWO GUARDS. WHAT'S YOUR NAME?
UH... OH, I'M NOBODY, MA'AM. A NOBODY.

WOULD YOU LIKE US TO SHOW YOU AROUND? IT'S A BIG PLACE.
I APPRECIATE THE OFFER, BUT NO, THANK YOU.

WHEW!
MUST BE THAT PIGDOM PRINCESS WE HEARD ABOUT. LOOKS LIKE SHE'S JOINED FORCES WITH THE CHIEF!

TROTTERS GAVE YOU A PASS?
WHEN HE WAS LUCID, YES. WHEN HE WASN'T THE OTHER, DARK TROTTERS...

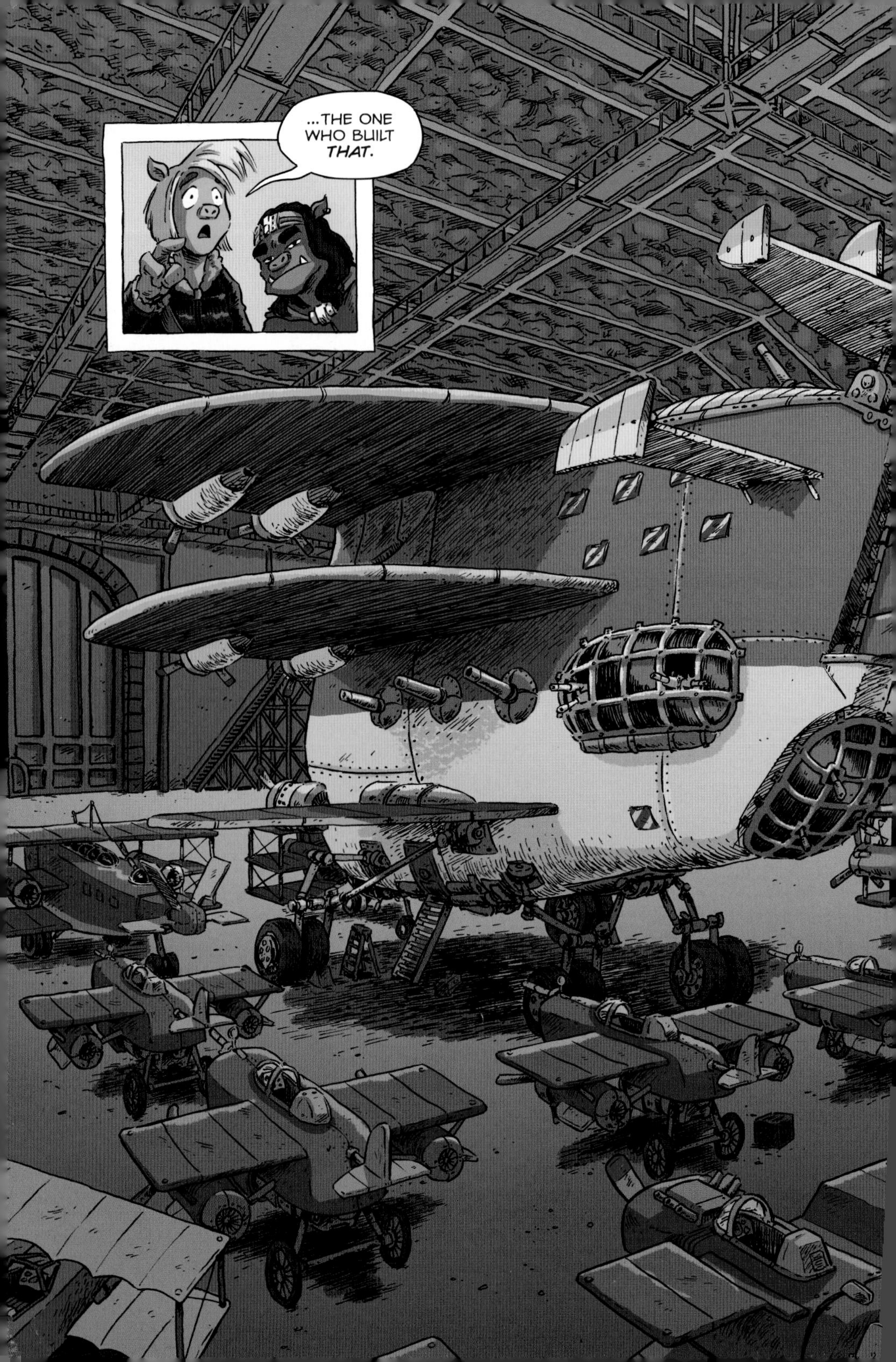
...THE ONE
WHO BUILT
THAT.

WHAT IS THAT *MONSTROSITY?*
TROTTERS'S *GREAT EXPERIMENT*... THE *FLYING FORTRESS.*
HE'S BUILT MANY DIFFERENT KINDS OF SKY CHARIOTS, FROM SMALL ONE-HOG VESSELS, TO GROUND RAIDERS LIKE THE *TUSKFIRE* AND *THIS* ENORMOUS *BEAST.*
THEY'RE ALL WAR MACHINES.

"TUSKFIRE"? THAT MUST BE THE ONE I SAW EATING PIGGLESWICK MARKET!
SHOULD WE TAKE THAT? OR THE FLYING FORTRESS? IT'D REDUCE TROTTERS'S INVASION FORCE BY HALF!
BOTH NEED CREWS AND THE MAGICSTRIX'S HELP TO GET THEM OFF THE GROUND.

CIRCE'S... "HELP"...? I DON'T UNDERSTAND.
THIS WAY, LADY LILY...
THE FORTRESS NEEDS THE POWER OF A SPELLBINDING CEREMONY FOR IT TO FLY.

ONLY CIRCE IS POWERFUL ENOUGH A MAGICAL ADEPT TO ACHIEVE SUCH A FEAT.
TROTTERS HAS THREATENED TO BURN THE TREASURES IN THE TEMPLE LIBRARY IF SHE DOESN'T HELP.

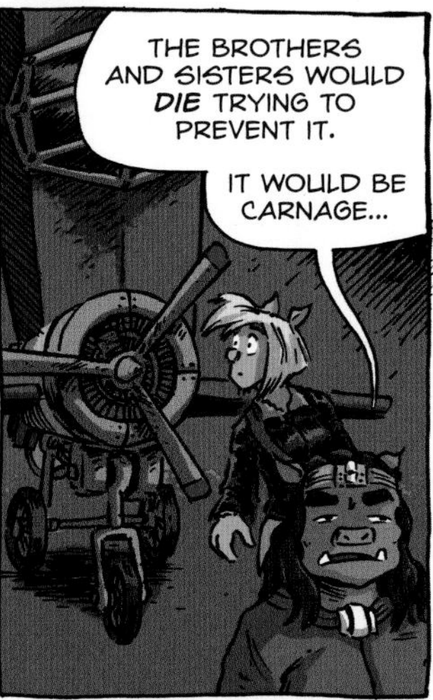
THE BROTHERS AND SISTERS WOULD DIE TRYING TO PREVENT IT.
IT WOULD BE CARNAGE...

AND CIRCE BELIEVES ANOTHER WAY TO NEUTRALIZE TROTTERS WILL COME. THE CIRCLE TOLD HER THAT MUCH.
ANOTHER WAY...?

oh BUNNYDROPS...!

THERE'S ESMERALDA!
ESMERALDA

SHE LOOKS ALL RIGHT. EVERYTHING'S *INTACT!*
Lady Lily...!

CHOM
CHOM
CHOM

HELLO, PIGGIKINS.
DON'T MOVE-- OR I'LL **FRY** YOU.

AND YOU, **DWARF PIG**-- OUT YOU COME.

I SUSPECTED YOU WEREN'T AS **COMPLIANT** TO MY WILL AS YOU **PRETENDED**, GRISELDA.
PARTNERING YOU WITH LILY HAS **SMOKED YOU OUT** INTO THE OPEN.

AND, MY DEAR LILY, DID YOU REALLY THINK I'D LET YOU GET AWAY TO WARN THE PIGDOM?
HAM, PLEASE LISTEN. YOU'RE NOT WELL. YOU'VE BEEN TAKEN OVER BY SOMETHING...

...YOU DON'T KNOW WHAT YOU'RE DOING!
ON THE CONTRARY... I KNOW EXACTLY WHAT I'M DOING.

SHRAAAAK
OH, I FORGOT. YOU'RE NOT SO PROUD THAT YOU WON'T USE MAGIC SHIELDING, EH?
NO!
JUST HAVE TO USE EXTRA POWER...!
SHRAAAAK

SHRAKDK
HAM! STOP IT, PLEASE!
THOOOM

YOUR RUDDER IS BROKEN. YOU WON'T FLY NOW.
WHO CREATED THE PROTECTION SPELL ON YOUR AIRCRAFT?

NOHOG YOU KNOW.
TELL ME! I WANT TO KNOW HOW IT COULD BE THAT STRONG.

I'LL FIND OUT, ANYWAY. BUT IF YOU TELL ME NOW, NOHOG WILL SUFFER.
ENOUGH.

TROTTERS, YOU STILL NEED MY COOPERATION FOR THE BINDING CEREMONY.
AND I WILL NOT GIVE IT IF THIS VILE COERCION CONTINUES.

DO NOT PROVOKE ME, CIRCE...
CHIEF...

THE CREWS ARE HERE. TIME FOR YOUR SPEECH.

OF COURSE!
THROW THOSE TWO IN A CELL, PHINEAS. WE'LL FIGURE OUT WHAT TO DO WITH THEM LATER.
DESTINY AWAITS!

MY FELLOWS... MY FRIENDS.
IT HAS BEEN A LONG ROAD.
YOU HAVE ENDURED HUNGER AND HARDSHIP.
YOU HAVE BEEN NEAR THE EDGE OF EXTINCTION...YOU LOOKED DEEP INTO THE ABYSS.
BUT THEN YOU LISTENED TO A STRANGER IN YOUR MIDST.
YOU HONORED ME BY HEARING MY PLANS AND PUTTING THEM INTO ACTION.
TOGETHER, WE HELD FAST. WE SURVIVED BY TOILING AS ONE.
OVER THE MOUNTAINS IS A LAND LUSH WITH RICHES, A TERRITORY WHOSE SOFT UNDERBELLY IS RIPE WITH FAT FOR ROASTING.
AND NOW WE ARE AT THE DAWN OF A NEW AGE.
WE NEED NEVER GO HUNGRY AGAIN. IT IS OURS FOR THE TAKING.
YOU ALL KNOW THE PLAN...
LET THE INVASION OF THE PIGDOM PLAINS BEGIN!
IT DOESN'T NEED TO BE THIS WAY.

WELL, WHAT ARE YOU WAITING FOR, CIRCE? LET'S GET STARTED!

THE SPELLBINDING CEREMONY... NOW YOU'LL SEE WHAT POWERFUL MAGIC REALLY IS.

IN THE HEAT VELDT, WE KNOW SOMETHING OF MAGIC, TOO. BUT IT SEEMS SO MUCH MORE POWERFUL IN THIS PLACE.

WHEN I FIRST ARRIVED IN THIS CITADEL AS A "GUEST" OF TROTTERS, I WAS SHUNNED.
NOT OUT OF CRUELTY, MORE OUT OF EMBARRASSMENT. BECAUSE, SUDDENLY, I WAS VISIBLE, A REPRESENTATIVE OF EVERYTHING THAT WAS BEING STOLEN FROM AFAR, HERE IN THE WARTHOGS' MIDST.

I'M A REMINDER OF WHAT THE WARTHOGS' SURVIVAL TACTICS COST.
BUT CIRCE AND HER FOLLOWERS ALWAYS SHOWED ME FRIENDSHIP.

FOR ALL HER POWER, CIRCE ALWAYS PUTS KINDNESS AND CONSIDERATION BEFORE OTHER CONCERNS.

THHRMMMM
LILY, NEVER, EVER MISTAKE KINDNESS FOR WEAKNESS.

MWOWMWOWMWOWMWOWMWOWMWOWMWOWMWOW

WOWMWOWMWOWMWOWMWOWMWOWMWOW

THRMMMM
YESSSSS.

MWO
WOWMWOWMWOWMWOWMW
THRMMM
SHRAAAAK

WHAT'S HAPPENING?
I DON'T KNOW.

FEEL THAT, CIRCE? DID YOU FEEL THE FLUX IN POWER? IT MOVED... FROM YOU TO ME!
FOOLISH SWINE! THAT'S NOT WHAT IT WAS...

RRRMMMMMMMMMM

PAH!
I DON'T NEED YOU ANYMORE!
NO!

RRRMMMMMMMMMMMMMMMMM

I CAN FEEL POWER COURSING THROUGH MY VEINS...

COME, PHINEAS, OBELIA...
DESTINY AWAITS!

WHAT HAVE YOU DONE?
OBELIA... SPEAK TO ME!

SHE'S ALIVE.
PHINEAS, I NEED YOU ON THE BRIDGE OF THE FLYING FORTRESS.
WE NEED HER, TOO!

SHE'S NOT GOING ANYWHERE. WE'LL MAKE DO. COME ON... SHE'LL BE FINE!
DESTINY AWAITS!

THRRRM
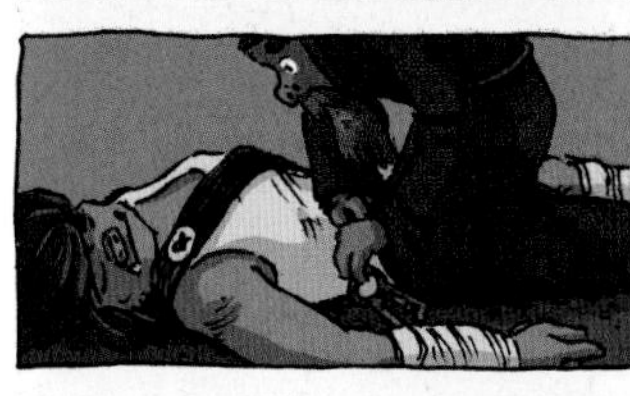

WELL DONE, LINUS!
WE MUST HELP THE MOST HIGH. SHE'S HURT.

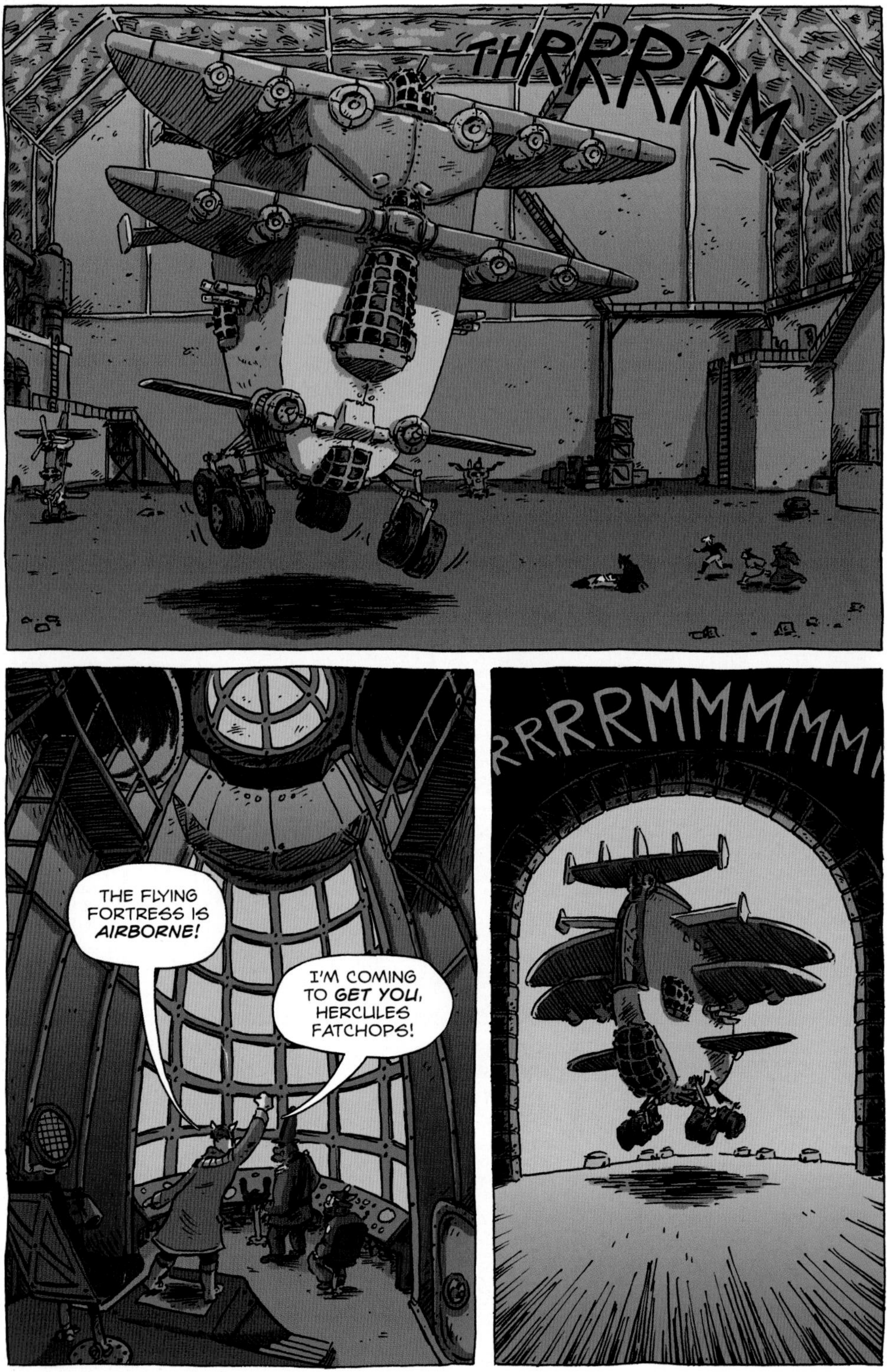

THRRRRM

THE FLYING FORTRESS IS **AIRBORNE!**
I'M COMING TO **GET YOU**, HERCULES FATCHOPS!

RRRRMMMMMM

MOST HIGH...?
I must speak with *Lady Lily*...
I-- I'M HERE, CIRCE...

You must *follow* them, Lily. You must *stop* Trotters... for all our sakes.
HE *DAMAGED* MY AIRCRAFT. SHE *CAN'T FLY*.

No... *look*...
BUT I *SAW*-- THERE WERE *HOLES* IN THE WINGS AND THE RUDDER...
MOST HIGH! DURING THE *SPELLBINDING*...?

Yes. Patched her up. Trotters... too *busy* to notice.
You are refueled from your own supplies. Remember, my enhancements are *magical*-- they won't last *forever*. But they'll hold for today...
THAT'S ALL WE NEED. JUST *TODAY*.

Griselda...?
I'M GOING TOO, MOST HIGH. I CAN *HELP* LADY LILY.

Then I must make you *safe*...
...Linus, give them each talismans...
TO WISH YOU *SAFETY* ON YOUR JOURNEY!

THANK YOU. I HAD ONE JUST LIKE IT...
MOST HIGH, *NO!* YOU'RE TOO WEAK...
WOWM WOWM

MOST HIGH...! CIRCE!
GO. I WILL ATTEND TO HER.
hhhhhh

MAY I BORROW YOUR WATER?

WHA--?
SPLOOSH!

WAKEY-WAKEY!
YOU'RE GOING TO TELL US WHAT HAM'S FLIGHT PATH IS.

WHAT...?
THEY'RE GONE, HONEY.

NO!
YES. YOUR BOARFRIEND AND YOUR PRECIOUS CHIEF LEFT YOU BEHIND.

I WON'T ASK TWICE. WHAT'S THEIR HEADING?

THEY'RE HEADING INTO THE PIGDOM VIA THE SNAGJAW PASS.
LOCK HER UP, AGATHA.

SNAGJAW PASS...?
SHORTEST ROUTE OVER THE MOUNTAINS, BUT TREACHEROUS AND OFTEN OBSCURED BY CLOUDS.

HERE...
I KNOW IT. WE CALL IT THE ALLFATHER'S PASS IN THE PIGDOM. IT'S A DIFFERENT ROUTE FROM THE ONE I CAME IN THROUGH...

LOOKS LIKE IT'S THE SAME ROUTE THEY USED WHEN THEY DID THEIR FIRST SCOUTING RUN. WHICH WILL TAKE THEM RIGHT OVER...

...MY HOUSE...

Linus... get me to the Temple. There is something else I must do...
MOST HIGH, YOU MUST REST...

HERE-- SPARE PAIR OF GOGGLES. YOU'LL NEED THEM UP THERE.
I WILL SEE YOU IN THE SKY, LADY LILY. I WILL WATCH YOUR BACK.

I'LL MAKE YOU A DEAL. WE BOTH COME OUT OF THIS ALIVE, WILL YOU STOP CALLING ME "LADY LILY"...?

DEAL. I WILL THINK OF SOMETHING APPROPRIATE...
TAKE GOOD CARE, CHILDREN...

RRRMMMMM

FAREWELL, CIRCE...
I SWEAR, I'LL RETURN...

THE EYE MAY SHOW US LILY AND GRISELDA'S JOURNEY.
I PRAY WE ENCOUNTER NO INTERFERENCE THIS TIME.
MOST HIGH, PLEASE SLOW DOWN...

AND THERE IS SOMETHING ELSE-- SOMEONE ELSE I MUST TRY TO CONTACT...

HEAR ME...

WE HAVE TO CATCH UP TO THEM BEFORE THEY GET TO THE SNAGJAW PASS!

...Because we'll lose them in those clouds...
COME ON NOW, ESMERALDA. I KNOW YOU'VE BEEN THROUGH A LOT, BUT YOU'RE TOUGH!

LET'S APPLY SOME OF THE ADVANTAGES OF SCIENCE...
RRRMMMMMM

WWWRRRRRRR

CLOUDS OVER THE SNAGJAW PASS, CHIEF.
SO I SEE.
THEO, LIGHT UP THE REAR LANTERNS SO THAT THE REST OF THE FLOTILLA CAN FOLLOW US THROUGH, SAFELY.
YES, CHIEF.

...WE'RE GOING FIRST.

CHIEF!

PCHOOOM
PCHOOOM
SPLAT
NOOOO!

FWUP

LILY.
AND ONE OTHER.

ALL SKY CHARIOTEERS! HEAR ME...
DO NOT BREAK FORMATION!

WE ARE BEING ATTACKED BY TWO ENEMY AIRCRAFT-- TWO PIG CHARIOTS. THEY'RE TRYING TO BREAK US UP BEFORE WE REACH THE PASS, BUT WE'RE NEARLY THERE...
KEEP FOLLOWING THE FLYING FORTRESS THROUGH.

REAR ESCORTS THREE, FOUR, AND FIVE, I NEED YOU TO PEEL AWAY AND ENGAGE THOSE GNATS!
ALL GUN EMPLACEMENTS-- GIVE SUPPORTING FIRE.

SHOOT THEM DOWN!
THIS IS A TOTAL *MISMATCH*. THERE'S JUST *TOO MANY* OF THEM.

THEY ARE BOTH **BETTER AT FLYING** THAN ANY OF TROTTERS'S WARRIORS, MOST HIGH... BUT THEY ARE HOPELESSLY **OUTNUMBERED.**
WE MUST **BELIEVE** IN LILY.

HEAR ME...

S'POSE I ALWAYS KNEW THAT THIS **WHOLE TRIP** WAS ONE, LONG ACT OF **DESPERATION...**

LET'S TRY A LITTLE GAME OF "CHICKEN," HAM...

WHAT-- WHAT'S SHE DOING?
SHE **CAN'T**... SHE **WOULDN'T**...

SHE CAN'T BE!
EVASIVE ACTION!

EH? WHICH WAY?
PORT, STARBOARD, I DON'T CARE!
DO IT NOW!

EEEEOOOOW!

NOOOOOOO
WROOWWWM
FCHOOM!
THAKOOM!

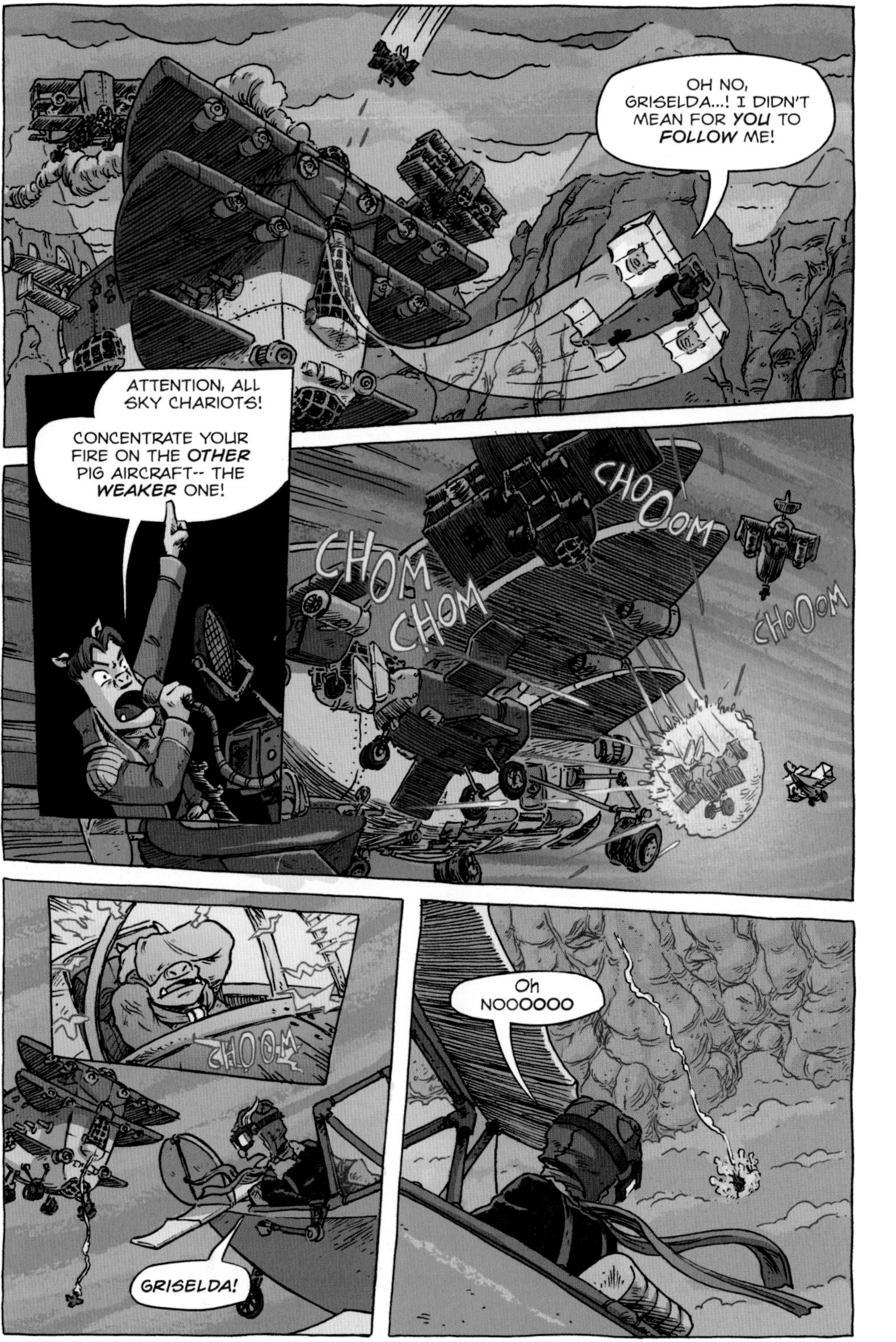

OH NO, GRISELDA...! I DIDN'T MEAN FOR *YOU* TO *FOLLOW* ME!

ATTENTION, ALL SKY CHARIOTS!

CONCENTRATE YOUR FIRE ON THE *OTHER* PIG AIRCRAFT-- THE *WEAKER* ONE!

CHOOOM

CHOM CHOM

CHOOOM

INTERFERENCE. THE EYE IS CLOUDING...
ONE DOWN!
SKY CHARIOTS-- CONCENTRATE FIRE ON THE SECOND PIG AIRCRAFT.
CHIEF, WE'RE ABOUT TO ENTER THE PASS!
YES, THAT IS THE PLAN!
WHAT, TWO SKY CHARIOTS, AT THE SAME TIME?
WE CAN'T BOTH FIT! WE HAVE TO GO THROUGH THE PASS SINGLE FILE!
KR-A-A-AAK
TUSKFIRE, YOU'RE OFF COURSE! DECREASE SPEED!
NO TIME TO CORRECT--

TUSKFIRE, KEEP YOUR HEIGHT! WE'LL BE THROUGH IN A FEW MOMENTS...
CAN'T KEEP HER NOSE UP...!
LILY LEANCHOPS...
THIS IS ALL YOUR FAULT!

THIS IS IT, ISN'T IT...?
I'M FLYING BLIND. I CAN'T GET OUT OF THIS.

DAD... I'M SORRY...

I'M SORRY I'LL NEVER SEE YOU AGAIN. I'M SORRY THAT I'M AS STUBBORN AS YOU!
BUT YOU AND MAMA MADE ME THIS WAY...!

SASHA, ARCHIE... I'M SORRY...
I MUST'VE BEEN CRAZY TO LEAVE YOU... I MISS YOU BOTH SO MUCH...

CIRCE, I'M SORRY I LET YOU DOWN...
GRISELDA...

OH, GRISELDA, I'M SO SORRY...
I SHOULD NEVER HAVE ASKED YOU TO COME WITH ME...

...OR YOU'LL NEVER MAKE IT ***OUT OF THE PASS!***

HIGH ONE, THE IMAGE IS ***RETURNING.*** LILY IS ***THROUGH!***

IF THEY'RE ON SCHEDULE, WE SHOULD BE SEEING THE SIGNAL FLARE TO INVADE...
ANY MOMENT...

...NOW...

BKROOOM

UH...
CHANGE OF PLAN...?

RRRRRRRRRMMMMMMMMM

NOW **HEAR THIS**... ALL WARTHOG AIRCRAFT...!
SHOOT DOWN THAT PIG CHARIOT. **SHOOT IT DOWN NOW!**

WE'RE IN THE **OPEN** NOW-- AND I **KNOW** YOU, HAM TROTTERS. YOU'RE GOING TO COME AT ME...

...LIKE A **SWARM**.

WAIT... HOW MANY AIRCRAFT HAS HAM GOT?
LOOK AT HER! SHE'S INSANE! SHE'S GOING TO GET SWATTED OUT OF THE SKY, BUT SHE'S HEADING STRAIGHT FOR US!
YOU HAVE TO ADMIRE HER COURAGE. SHE NEVER GIVES--

uuuup
BCHOOOM

WHA... HAPPENED?
WE WERE ATTACKED FROM THE REAR.

WE'RE LOSING ALTITUDE. NEED TO CORRECT OUR COURSE...
FROM THE REAR? BY WHAT...?

BY THOSE.

NO! IT CAN'T BE!
Oh, SKY BUNNIES! DAD, YOU DID IT!
WE HAVE BEEN HEARD!

LILY, CAN YOU HEAR ME? ARE YOU ALL RIGHT?
DAD! Oh, I'VE NEVER BEEN SO ALL RIGHT!

CAN YOU JOIN US?
NO. TOO MANY OF HAM'S FORCES BETWEEN YOU AND ME...

AND I'VE ALREADY PICKED UP A HANGER-ON...
HOLD ON, LILY. WE'LL GET TO YOU AS FAST AS WE CAN.

THAT'S HIM. I KNOW IT IS! IT'S HERCULES FATCHOPS! EVEN THE WAY HE FLIES IS ARROGANT...
HE MUST'VE SWALLOWED HIS PRIDE AND USED MAGIC TO BUILD THIS FLEET SO QUICKLY!

WARTHOGS, CONCENTRATE YOUR FIRE ON THE LEAD PIG AIRCRAFT...
CHIEF, WE'RE TAKING A PUMMELING HERE!
THEY CAME OUT OF NOWHERE!

CHIEF, WE NEED TO FALL BACK, REGROUP.
OUR SURPRISE ATTACK ISN'T MUCH OF A SURPRISE!

PHINEAS, SET COURSE FOR THE LEAD PIG AIRCRAFT. I'LL MAN THE MAIN GUNS MYSELF.
CHIEF...!

DO IT!

WHOEVER HE IS, I CAN'T *SHAKE* HIM.
AND I CAN'T EVEN GET CLOSE TO THE OTHER PIGDOM AIRCRAFT...

CHOM CHOM
WHO'S THAT?!
THANK YOU, WHOEVER YOU ARE!

GRISELDA!
OH, I'M SO *HAPPY* TO SEE Y--
AAACK.
KEEP YOUR MIND ON THE JOB, LILY...!
PCHOW

MOST HIGH, IS THERE ANY WAY WE CAN *HELP* THEM?
IT IS *FAR*, AND I AM *WEAK*... I MUST SAVE MY ENERGY FOR *COMMUNICATION*...
THIS WILL *PLAY OUT* THE WAY IT *MUST*...

ALL UNITS! CONCENTRATE YOUR FIRE ON THE *BIGGEST* WARTHOG AIRCRAFT!
UNHOLY PIGSKINS! LOOKS LIKE THE BIG SHIP WANTS *MY* HIDE...
BRAKKA-BRAKKA-BRAKKA
BET I KNOW WHO'S *ON BOARD* IT.

EEEEEYOWWWWW
BRAKKA-
BRAKKA-

CHIEF! YOU'RE SHOOTING UP OUR OWN AIRCRAFT!
THEY'RE IN THE WAY.
YOU'RE CRAZY!

NO. I SEE THE BIGGER PICTURE...
BIGGER REWARDS. NOTHING MUST GET IN MY WAY.

ENOUGH!
NOOOOO!
DAD!
THE TRICKBOX...!

MMROOOWWW
IF I CAN JUST GET CLOSE ENOUGH...
YOU CAN'T FIRE ON OUR OWN AIRCRAFT!
OOOOOF!
MMROOOOOW
MMROOOOOOOOW
LILY...!
AAAAARRGH
THERE'S ALWAYS A BIGGER PICTURE, YOU MORONIC, DOG-FACED FOOL!
LET ME HELP YOU SEE IT...
ZRRRKKK

RRRMMMWWROOWW

HOLD ON...
HOLD ON...!
...STRENGTH, LILY!
KTHUMMMMM

WRRRRROOOOOW

Uh-oh.

CHUF

KCHUK-KCHUK

COME ON, KEEP YOUR NOSE **UP**, ESMERALDA...

Whew

YAY!
HOORAY!
YAY!
YAY!
HOORAY!
WAIT. IT IS NOT **OVER**...

Oooooh...

HALT!
IDENTIFY YOURSELF!

HERCULES.
HERCULES FATCHOPS.
I'VE WAITED A VERY LONG TIME FOR THIS MOMENT.
EH...?

STAND DOWN, SOLDIER. D'YOU KNOW WHO THAT IS?
THAT'S LILY LEANCHOPS, HERCULES FATCHOPS'S DAUGHTER, ALSO KNOWN AS AERIAL HONKER...!

MA'AM!
What...?
IT'S ALL RIGHT, LILY. THE WHOLE PIGDOM KNOWS. I'M AFRAID A REPORTER LEAKED YOUR-- ER, "SECRET IDENTITY"...!
YEAH, YOU'RE FAMOUS!

YOU WOULDN'T BELIEVE WHAT'S HAPPENED IN THE LAST COUPLE OF DAYS...
ARCHIE! SASHA...? HOW CAN YOU BE HERE?

A FRIEND GUIDED US-- CIRCE. I'VE BEEN IN COMMUNICATION WITH HER VIA THE NETWORK OF THE MYSTIC CIRCLES. SHE TIPPED US OFF TO HAM TROTTERS'S PLANS...!
MRS. WIGGSLY AND HER SON ARE OUR CONSULTANTS ON MAGIC...

OKAY-- WHAT? THAT'S LOVELY, AND I'M OVERJOYED TO SEE YOU, BUT WE HAVE TO GET TO MY DAD...!
LILY, WAIT...!

NO TIME.
LILY!
ARCHIE, STOP RIGHT NOW! DO YOU HEAR ME?

LIKE MINDS ACROSS THE MOUNTAINS HEARD YOU, HIGH ONE.
THEY DID, INDEED!
BE CAREFUL, LILY. THERE IS STILL GREAT DANGER...

HAM TROTTERS!
I SUPPOSE IT HAD TO BE YOU, DIDN'T IT? YOU ALWAYS DID OVERUSE MAGIC...

...DON'T WANT TO HEAR IT.
NO!
AAAH!
ZRAAAAK

SORRY...

THAT THE BEST YOU'VE GOT?
WHAT'S THIS? SORCERY...?

NOT SORCERY, NOT MAGIC-- SCIENCE.
HOGWASH! I JUST BLEW YOU OUT OF THE SKY...

INDEED-- THROUGH SHEER FORCE, OLD BOY. HAD NO MEANS OF DEFLECTING IT.
THIS DEVICE IS SOMETHING I RIGGED UP AT EVEN SHORTER NOTICE THAN THE PIGDOM'S AIRCRAFT FLEET.
IT'S DESIGNED TO EITHER DEFLECT OR STORE AND REROUTE MAGICAL ENERGY...

...LIKE SO.

HMM. HERE ON THE GROUND, I THINK WE'RE A BIT MORE EVENLY MATCHED...

I ALWAYS TRIED TO TEACH YOU NOT TO BLUDGEON WHEN A MERE TAP WILL DO.
NO! YOU NEVER KNEW ANYTHING ABOUT MAGIC!

NOT SO. MY SISTER SASHA IS A MAGICAL ADEPT. I LEARNED A FEW TRICKS GROWING UP WITH HER...
SHE, AND A WHOLE TEAM OF CARPENTERS AND MAGICAL ADEPTS, HELPED ME ASSEMBLE THE FLEET THAT INTERCEPTED YOU.

THAT'S TEAMWORK, DEAR BOY.
THIS IS SCIENCE.
SCIENCE!

SCIENCE AND MAGIC COEXIST. MAYBE A BALANCE OF BOTH IS DESIRABLE.
MY DAUGHTER TAUGHT ME THAT.

I'LL KILL YOU WITH MY BARE HANDS!

AAARGH!

DIIIIIE!

AAAAaaack
SHRAAK

ENOUGH!
Enough, now.

KSSSSSSSS
SKRAP
BY THE ALLFATHER!
WHAT IS IT...?

DARKNESS MADE MANIFEST! AS BEFORE, A THING NOT OF THE NOW...
WE MUST HELP HER. SEND STRENGTH, BROTHERS AND SISTERS...

GUARDIANS OF THE CIRCLE, I INVOKE THEE. THY STRENGTH, THY GRACE, THY IMAGE, THY LAW IS MINE.
BY THE FOUR CARDINALS, BY WING AND BY HOOF...
...BY STONE AND BY SKY...

I COMMAND THEE, AWAY AND CONSUME THYSELF.
THERE IS NO PLACE FOR YOU HERE.
KRSHOOOM 
BEGONE!

WHERE DID IT GO...?
BACK TO WHERE IT CAME FROM, I HOPE.
IT... THAT *THING* WAS INSIDE HAM! *CONTROLLING* HIM...
LILY!

MY BRAVE, BEAUTIFUL DAUGHTER!
I'M SORRY I *DIDN'T LISTEN.* I SHOULD *ALWAYS* LISTEN TO YOU. YOU'RE MORE *PRECIOUS* TO ME THAN ANYTHING ELSE IN THIS WORLD!

IS HE ALIVE?
HE'LL SURVIVE.
GOOD. HE'S GOT A LOT TO *ANSWER* FOR.

OR PERHAPS THE *DARKNESS* THAT *POSSESSED* HIM HAS, PHINEAS.
WE WILL FIND THE ANSWERS TOGETHER.
CIRCE...! MOST HIGH, I'M SO *ASHAMED. FORGIVE ME* FOR TURNING AWAY FROM YOU...

YOU NEED TO SIGNAL YOUR FORCES...
TELL THEM TO *SURRENDER* AND ALLOW THEMSELVES TO BE ESCORTED TO THE PIGDOM'S AIR BASE.

WE HAVE A LOT TO *TALK* ABOUT.
I *AGREE.*
IF ANYTHING, THIS AFFAIR IS A DEMONSTRATION OF HOW PIGS AND WARTHOGS MUST NOW *COMMUNICATE.*

WE CAN OVERCOME ANY DIFFERENCES. WE CAN WORK TOGETHER, AS ONE, FOR ALL HOGKIND...
Things'll never be the same again...

Price: 2 ½ PP

Pearlday, Hogtween 17th,

The Pigdom Plains Post

PEACE IN OUR TIME

PIGDOM LEADERS MEET WARTHOG REPRESENTATIVES

Hercules Fatchops introduces Pigminister Franklin Flanksford to Sister Circe, Magicstrix and High Bibliotaph of the Celestial Temple of the Skypigs.

The INVASION was all a mistake, assures CIRCE, LEADER of the WARTHOGS

By our roving correspondents,
Patrick Hamkins and Carla Gruntfuzz

History was made yesterday when CIRCE, ruler of the Warthog territory known to extend north of the mountains beyond our sovereign nation of the Pigdom Plains, paid a visit to Port Porkins and our Pigminister Prime Franklin Flanksford. She brought with her representatives of her land and gifts for all who attended the occasion, which Deputy Chompton called "a celebration—a time to rejoice."

"SHE INSISTED THAT PIGKIND AND THE WARTHOGS ARE JUST BRANCHES OF THE SAME TREE. 'WE HAVE SO MUCH TO LEARN FROM ONE ANOTHER.' AIRCRAFT WILL BE BUILT TO FORGE CLOSER LINKS WITH THE LONG-DEMONIZED WARTHOG TERRITORY..."

URP

AH, LILY...! THAT PROPOSAL TO BUILD A STATUE OF YOU NEEDS YOUR APPROVAL.
AS I ALREADY TOLD YOU TWENTY TIMES, MR. SLUDGEWELL...

NO STATUES. SPEND THE MONEY ON SOMETHING USEFUL.
AH, YES, WELL, THERE'S ALSO THIS ISSUE OF THE DESIGN CONSULTANCY...

WE NEED YOUR HELP TO BUILD THESE NEW AIRCRAFT!
ASK MY FATHER.

BUT LILY... YOU'RE THE SOURCE!
WHOOOPS

IT'S A WHOLE NEW WORLD, ISN'T IT?
YES.

YOUR FATHER'S HAPPY.
HE LOVES A BIG PROJECT. THERE'S TALK OF TRADE AGREEMENTS AND EXCHANGES BETWEEN THE PIGDOM AND THE WARTHOGS...

YES, HE'S ALREADY BUTTING HEADS WITH THE PIGMINISTER PRIME ABOUT HOW TO HANDLE IT ALL. SLUDGEWELL'S BACKING HIM UP! HE'S GOT A NEW BEST FRIEND.
WELL, I'M GLAD CIRCE REQUESTED YOU AS A LIAISON. YOU'LL TALK SOME SENSE INTO THEM.

AND HOW ARE YOU?

YOU'VE BEEN VERY QUIET EVER SINCE YOU CAME BACK...

IT'S YOUR FRIEND, ISN'T IT? GRISELDA...?
MM.

SHE DIDN'T COME BACK. SHE WAS SUPPOSED TO COME HERE WITH ME, TO THE PIGDOM...
I KNOW I SAW HER... SHE SAVED MY LIFE.

I'M SURE SHE TRIED TO FLY BACK **HOME**, WHILE SHE HAD THE **CHANCE**...
SHE'S OUT THERE **SOMEWHERE**...

SASHA, I SAW THINGS UP THERE THAT I CAN'T **EXPLAIN**. BUT SOMEHOW, THEY **MADE SENSE**.
NONE OF THIS, DOWN HERE, MAKES **ANY** SENSE TO ME.

THEY'RE ALL FALLING OVER THEMSELVES TO BE **A PART** OF THIS **BRAVE NEW WORLD**.

WITHOUT **YOU**, THEY WOULDN'T BE SO **INSPIRED**, LILY.
WITHOUT GRISELDA, **I** WOULDN'T BE HERE.

I NEED TO GO AND LOOK FOR HER. I NEED TO **FIND OUT**.
I **KNOW**.

BUT PLEASE **COME BACK** TO US. I DON'T THINK I COULD BEAR TO **LOSE** YOU.
I WILL.

THIS IS MY **HOME BASE** WITH MY **CHIEF ENGINEER!**
ESMERALDA II IS READY TO **GO!**
HER FIRST **TEST FLIGHT!** WHERE SHALL I TAKE HER...?

NEXT TIME WE'RE GOING TO BUILD ONE SO *I* CAN GO UP, TOO!
NOT YET, YOU'RE NOT.

LILY NEEDS A GOOD TEAM AT "*HOME BASE.*" YOU CAN BE SATISFIED WITH BEING ***CHIEF ENGINEER*** FOR ***NOW***-- UNTIL YOU'RE A BIT OLDER...

AW, ***MOTHER***...

THERE'LL BE ***PLENTY OF TIME*** FOR ***ADVENTURES***, YOU'LL SEE...!

YEAH, YOU'RE RIGHT...

I'LL JUST HAVE TO BIDE MY TIME...!

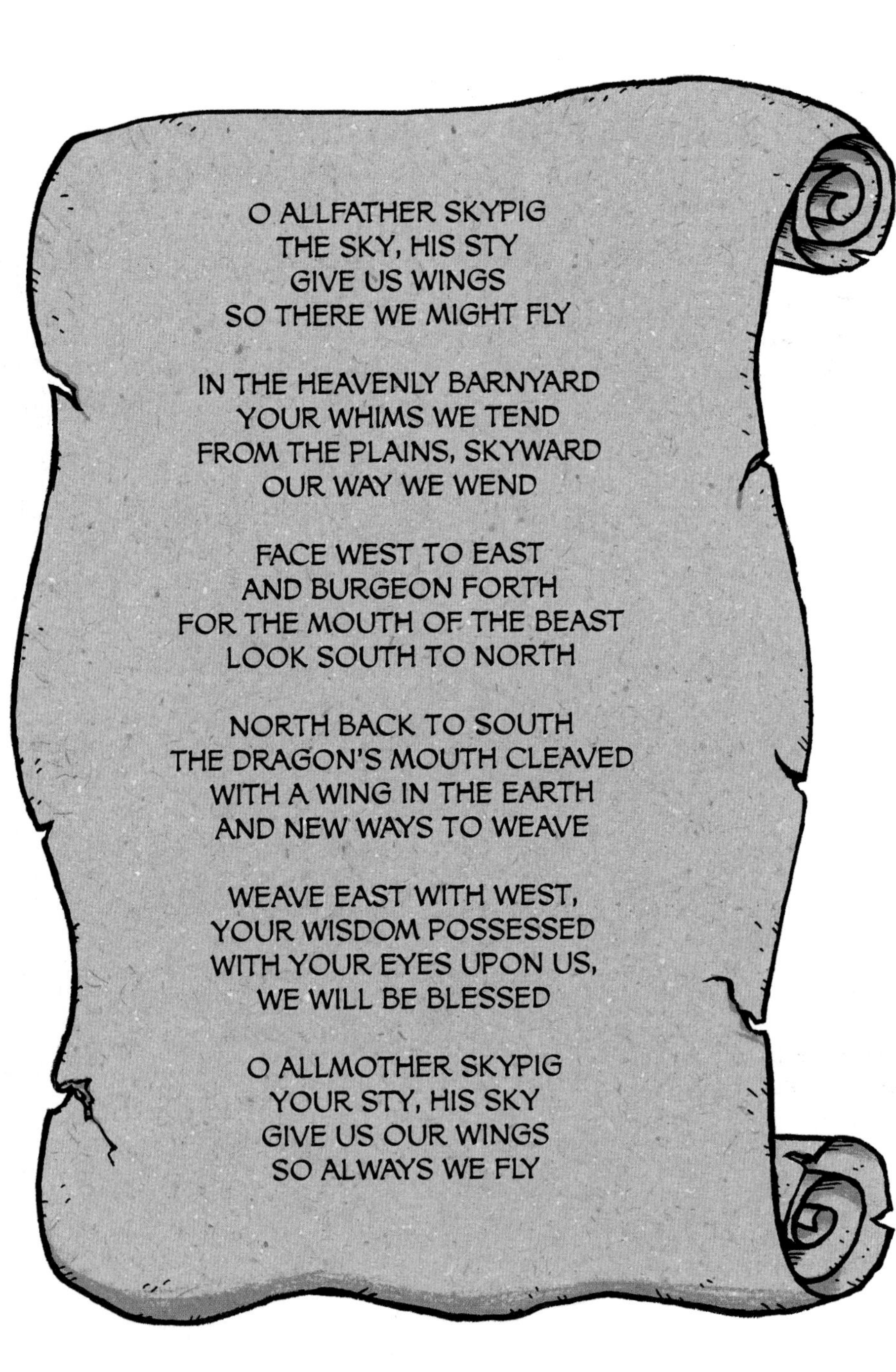
O ALLFATHER SKYPIG
THE SKY, HIS STY
GIVE US WINGS
SO THERE WE MIGHT FLY

IN THE HEAVENLY BARNYARD
YOUR WHIMS WE TEND
FROM THE PLAINS, SKYWARD
OUR WAY WE WEND

FACE WEST TO EAST
AND BURGEON FORTH
FOR THE MOUTH OF THE BEAST
LOOK SOUTH TO NORTH

NORTH BACK TO SOUTH
THE DRAGON'S MOUTH CLEAVED
WITH A WING IN THE EARTH
AND NEW WAYS TO WEAVE

WEAVE EAST WITH WEST,
YOUR WISDOM POSSESSED
WITH YOUR EYES UPON US,
WE WILL BE BLESSED

O ALLMOTHER SKYPIG
YOUR STY, HIS SKY
GIVE US OUR WINGS
SO ALWAYS WE FLY

For Nadia

Thank you, Angela Watson and all the Abadzis family for your love and support. I'm not me without you. Thanks to Ed, Nikki, Cas, John, Luciana, Alan, Glenn, Wallis, Rachael, Steve, Josh, Jim, Sean, and Gary for all the distance management and for being you. Thanks to Kirsty for all the good sense and to Sally for still being the best listening ear.

Special thanks also to Kevin, Melissa, Garth, Ruth, Charlie, Jaime, Jon, Alex, Si, Greg, other Greg, Sebastian, and Jules for being there. Big thanks to Lewis for the portrait.

Very special thanks to Jerel and Mark, who believed a pig can-fly.

—Nick Abadzis

Lewis Trondheim and Brigitte Findakly

Thanks to Jesse Lonergan, Roho, Kimball Anderson, and the wonderful comics community of the BCR.

Thanks to those always inspiring artists who make machines fly: Mattias Adolfsson, Charles A. A. Dellschau, Hayao Miyazaki, and Ian McQue.

Thanks to Laurel Lynn Leake and Alex Campbell for your marvelous talent and perseverance. Special thanks to Katie Armour, to all my friends, and to my loving family whose love and support carry me through.

And thanks to Nick and Mark, who opened up a whole new world to me.

—Jerel Dye

Jesse Lonergan

New York

Published by First Second
First Second is an imprint of Roaring Brook Press,
a division of Holtzbrinck Publishing Holdings Limited Partnership
175 Fifth Avenue, New York, New York 10010

Library of Congress Control Number: 2016945556

Paperback ISBN: 978-1-62672-086-2
Hardcover ISBN: 978-1-62672-743-4

First edition 2017
Printed in China by Toppan Leefung Printing Ltd., Dongguan City, Guangdong Province

Penciled with 2H Faber Castell 9000 Pencil and inked with Copic Multiliner SP pens on Strathmore Smooth Bristol paper. Colored digitally in Photoshop.

Paperback: 10 9 8 7 6 5 4 3 2 1
Hardcover: 10 9 8 7 6 5 4 3 2 1